# Tree of Shadow

## Dallin Chapman

*Dallin Chapman*

Newman Books

First published in Great Britain in 2016

By
Newman Books
45 Shipston Road
Stratford-upon-Avon
Warwickshire
CV37 7LN

Printed and bound in the UK by G H Smith & Son,
The Advertiser Office, Market Place, Easingwold, York, YO61 3AB.

ISBN 978-0-9558699-9-0

For Marcus, Richard and Joanna

# Chapter 1

Galen Nodeef stood in the forest clearing, his figure rooted in the soil. All day he had worked with the other men until early evening came and they laid down their tools. The careful cutting and replanting process allowed time for occasional chatter but today, to his comrades' surprise, Galen had not contributed to any conversation.

"You are quiet today, Galen?" Anton was one of the older men and his eyes held the younger man in the full depth of the question, so that Galen must respond truthfully or retreat into evasiveness, and to do the latter was contrary to the way of his people. He stopped working for a moment, brushing the bark from his hands. He could not disclose his thoughts.

"There is something on my mind, but it is like a distant cloud, scarcely formed. Allow me to say no more at present."

"It is not good to hold such thoughts; the mind will draw them closer and give them substance. If you cannot speak with me, please go to one of the Counsellors."

Galen hesitated. "I will visit my grandmother."

"Ah." Anton's response was neither smile nor sigh. "She is a woman of great wisdom, but remember, Galen, that her love for you may sometimes shelter you too much."

Anton moved away, touching Galen's hand briefly as he went. He had spoken and felt he could say no more. At forty, Galen was reaching full maturity and should be trusted to know where to turn for help. Galen watched him go. The gesture had moved the younger man and he opened his mouth to speak, but it was too late.

"Galen, come, help me carry this large log over to the pile." Young Matthew was standing next to him smiling, indicating the wood at their feet. The chanting was beginning, the celebration of the shared rhythm of labour, the song marking approaching rest. Like perfect echoes, other refrains wafted across the forest from distant workplaces. Galen raised his clear voice to join in, lifting the log with Matthew, nodding at comrades as they carried the wood to the pile. Even though all the men were similarly dressed in loose, white trousers and short, white jackets, with light black boots upon their feet, Galen's tumbling curls, blond almost to whiteness, and his unusual height, separated him from those around him.

The walk home in the early evening was usually one of the most pleasant times of day, as the men enjoyed each other's company and anticipated their homecoming, but tonight Galen hung back, telling the others to start off without him. He waited whilst their voices faded into the distance and he was alone. Slowly the place reclaimed its forest voice: the breathing of the wind in the great trees, the muted singing of birds and the rustle in the undergrowth of unseen life.

Galen leant his face against the trunk of an oak tree and placed his hands on the wood. He had to know. Surely to try and discover what lay on the other side would harm no-one? Until he knew the answer, there could be no rest. He drew away from the tree. Where his cheek had lain the wood was moist, and all through the forest sighs of other trees accompanied him as he started his journey home.

As Galen emerged from the forest, early evening burst upon him in a kaleidoscope of pinks and mauves. The way home lay ahead across undulating countryside, past streams and fields and the cultivated crops of his people. He was quite alone and he started to run, his boots making no sound, driven by a sudden need to see Anna and the children. For once he did not notice the beauty of the fields as he raced past, nor was he aware of the metamorphosis of the sky as purples and indigos swept in, bringing with them the darker shades of night. More than anything else, he must talk to his grandmother.

"Lie quietly, Galen, I will take care of you. You must have tripped and fallen, lost consciousness. The flesh on your hands is torn. Lie still whilst I bind the wounds."

It was almost dark when Galen reached the edge of the houses. He could smell scents of cooking as he walked along past the low, white dwellings set amongst open lawns. The Centre of Worship in the middle of the main square was silent for the moment, but from the sanctuary windows drifted sounds of voices. It was here that Anna had given birth to the children, and it was here that the old ones came to rest and prepare for their final journey. It was here that Galen's grandmother had taken him.

The doctor had been very surprised, for there were few accidents amongst the people and any small hurts were quickly healed.

"Why, Galen, these are very deep wounds. How did this come about, child?"

"I think I must have tripped and fallen. I can't remember. I must have lost consciousness."

"How did you fall, Galen?"

He had shaken his head. "I do not remember."

His grandmother had sat close by him whilst the doctor cleaned the wounds, pulled the flesh together and dressed his hands. As he drifted into sleep he had heard the two adults speaking in low voices.

"These are no ordinary cuts, sister, brought about by childhood energy. And I can find no injury to his head, so why should he lose consciousness? There is something

3

different about this, something I do not understand."

"Shush, the child will hear you. The wounds will heal, he will forget, it was nothing."

"If you have the smallest doubt you must go to one of the Counsellors."

"He is sleeping, let him rest, that is all he needs."

Yet the wounds had taken a long time to heal. Despite all the care from the doctors the flesh repeatedly burst open and bled afresh. Galen was feverish for days on end and tossed uneasily when he slept. He did not leave the sanctuary for a long time and, when finally he was thought fit enough to go home, the scars on his hands still ached when he was tired and interfered with his rest. But no-one talked to him about his accident again and, as the years ripened, memories of that day lay buried in the back of his mind.

Standing outside the entrance to the Centre of Worship in the evening dusk, Galen glanced at his hands; the scars were barely visible. It was thirty years since he had left the sanctuary and since then he had avoided going there whenever possible, although most of the people went regularly, taking gifts, sitting with the old ones, bringing the children to see the newly-born infants. He placed his hand upon the massive door. It swung open and he stood on the threshold, raising his eyes to the light that enveloped the interior. It seemed to emanate from the paintings on the walls and the roof that vaulted beyond eye's reach. In the centre stood the ancient table, lovingly sculpted from wood of the forest. The carvings on the table had been crafted by skilled hands, and the life of the people, the flow of the seasons, were depicted in delicate patterns on the surfaces. Two of the Counsellors stood beside it, their presence merging with the light so that their chanting seemed to be a part of the very air itself. Galen held out his arms and raised his voice, stepping across to join them, resting his hands on their shoulders.

The Counsellors smiled at him in welcome, but he did not know that at his touch they trembled, sensing for a brief moment the torn palms of the other man and the inexplicable nature of those wounds.

# Chapter 2

Anna was standing in the doorway, waiting for him. He took both her hands in the customary greeting, feeling the soft texture of her skin and the flow of love that ran from her fingers into his. They held each other's gaze for a long moment, then inclined their heads and raised them again before embracing, pressing their cheeks together, placing their lips in turn upon the other's forehead.

"The children are at the table, Galen, and the food is ready for you on the stove."

How fine she was with her delicate bones, her gracefulness, her soft voice. When he lay with her at night, the gentleness of her beauty was a continuing source of joy. Now he ran his hand over the fair hair cascading down her back, the gesture telling her that his lateness was unintentional, feeling her understanding as she led him to the kitchen.

Exclamations of pleasure greeted him as he entered the room. Rachel, with the enthusiasm of an eight-year-old, jumped down from her stool and held out her hands to him. Holding the fingers in his palms, he smiled into her eyes before bending to press his cheek to hers and exchange kisses upon the forehead. Then he lifted her into his arms and carried her to the table, where he placed her back on the stool.

"See, Father, what we have tonight from the food gathering." Nathan's hands were firm and warm, his blue eyes meeting his father's gaze with steady seriousness. Although only ten years old, the boy already had the marks of a Counsellor upon him. Galen dropped to his knees so that they could greet each other. When he had kissed the boy's forehead he rose to his feet.

"And what did you receive, Nathan?"

"I chose the cheese. Everyone had a piece. It will taste of the rich grasses. And mother fetched some herbs from the garden of the elders and the vegetables are…" He stopped, lost for words, his eyes glowing with anticipation. Galen laughed, his love for the child swelling in his heart.

"Come, let us share our meal," he cried, sniffing appreciatively at the smell rising from the great pot on the stove. They joined hands in a circle and lifted their heads. It was Anna who spoke the words in her clear, fluted voice:

"We taste the food of the earth
Like fruit for our souls,
Shared with the family
Of light in the light."

"Of light in the light," echoed Galen and the children. Anna ladled the smoking vegetables onto the platters, whilst Galen sliced the bread, crusty covered, soft textured within, baked that morning. They ate with quiet pleasure whilst they talked of the day's progress and the evening to come.

"After Worship, may we read from the Book of the Ancients," asked Rachel, "and hear the story of what happened right at the beginning?"

"Tonight I must go and see my grandmother but tomorrow, if you wish, we will leave at dawn and walk to the River and I will tell you the old story again." Galen spoke quite impulsively, but as soon as the words were uttered he felt a surge of anticipation and excitement at the thought of such an expedition.

"Oh, Galen," – Anna was smiling, but her eyes were quite grave – "do you think you should take the children on your own? I cannot come with you as I shall be with my parents."

"There can be no reason why the three of us should not

travel together. Nathan and Rachel will be safe with me, and on the way home they may come with me to the first food gathering and choose the ingredients for the day's meals." He swept his young son and daughter into his arms, smiling at Anna over their heads, feeling their delighted response.

"I am still not sure, Galen. Is it not wiser to travel with others?" He did not hear her above the children's excited chatter and she hesitated. Galen and the children looked so happy and they would not be gone too long. She let the matter rest.

They stepped into the evening air swathed in their cloaks, joining others also on their way to the Centre of Worship, until the broad pathway was filled with figures and murmurs of greetings. Although darkness had come, the Centre of Worship shone out in the night, drawing them towards it. No-one could see the top of the building, so intense was the light above, but the doors were flung open so that the people could flow through, flinging back their cloaks as they entered. The Counsellors stood waiting by the ancient table, arms outstretched in the gesture of welcome.

And still the people came, silent now, their concentration deepening the stillness, until the Counsellors slowly lowered their arms. Then the chanting began, rhythmic, hushed at first, until the Counsellors turned away from the multitude towards the table and the people lifted their voices in a mighty song.

Anna felt a faint fluttering of anxiety. It was such an unusual feeling that at first she did not recognise it. Her instinct was to go straight to one of the Counsellors, for since childhood all the teachings had guided her towards openness and sharing. Sitting with the Elders and Counsellors through her early years, she had always longed to learn, but yet she had also known that her achievements were part of a patterned whole and therefore alone they meant nothing.

Now she sat on her own awaiting Galen's return. All over the land the people would be sleeping; only Galen and his grandmother would be breaking the quiet of the night. Anna knew that, above all things, Galen's grandmother loved to talk with her grandson, and as she neared the time for her final journey she often did not sleep but kept watch, sitting in her chair by the window so that she could observe the stars. Galen had kept vigil with the old lady before, so why tonight should she feel a slight weight around her heart, quite alien to her, yet strangely recognisable? She had only experienced anything like this sensation once before, and that she had long since dismissed as youthful inexperience. It had been when she and Galen spontaneously joined hands in recognition that they wished to marry. Even as the warmth of Galen's hand enfolded hers, the pain had crept around her heart so that her initial joy was cut short and she had fallen down with a cry of bewilderment. Galen had lifted her and carried her to the Counsellors and, despite her request that he remain, he left her there to speak with them alone. The conversation, long since expunged from her memory, now stole back into her mind.

"Sister Anna, Galen is a fine young man, steeped in the teachings and stories of our people, a gifted child of the forest. Even here he is of a rare beauty of spirit. Yet we counsel you not to marry him, for his sake as well as yours."

"But, Father, why?"

"You may hardly remember, but when Galen was a boy of ten he had an accident. It is the first time that such a thing has happened amongst our people in this way. You know that the physicians can heal our hurts almost instantly. You visit the sanctuary regularly, Anna; what do you see there?"

"Why, the old ones or the mothers awaiting the birth of a child, or else gathering strength afterwards." She looked at the Counsellor with a puzzled frown.

"Yet Galen was there a long time whilst the doctors worked ceaselessly to heal his wounds. And in all that time he would never say how he sustained his injuries."

"Yes, but that is now quite…"

"You have been taught about fear, Anna, although, like most of our people, you have never fully experienced it. We are simple, yet that simplicity is profound; we retain it by understanding the things we must never be. When the doctors saw Galen's wounds, for the first time they sensed the presence of such things."

"I do not understand. What things?"

"Anna, Galen has been set apart amongst our people. If he is drawn too closely in, the wish to move further away may gather round him like his cloak."

"Oh, Father, surely marrying the woman he loves can only enhance his fine qualities?"

The old Counsellor looked long and keenly at Anna. Around him stood the other Counsellors, men and women of many ages, but it was he who questioned her with quiet and insistent love. Like all the young women in their community her face was moulded with an open lovingness, the calm generosity of their people. Yet in her was also a stronger need than others to share individual love, and it was this that the Counsellor saw and pondered upon. Throughout her schooling days this had been recognised and discussed by those who watched over her. It would not matter if any man other than Galen had loved her. But Galen and Anna? Since the accident Galen had been the focus of much quiet observation. Their intuition told the Counsellors that Galen should not marry, that the stirring of such love could be… dangerous…for him.

"Father?" Anna was awaiting his reply. The freedom to choose was central to their code, but choice was never lightly made. The mutual searching for the right choice was an accepted way of life, the reasons for a decision always understood. In their discussions the Counsellors had marvelled at the growing spirit of Galen, whilst at the same time sensing the tiniest breach in its perfection. Perhaps, after all, Anna would finally heal that breach.

"Sister, Galen and you have joined hands in love. All blessings upon you. But be a gentle watcher, Anna, and guard the spirit of your husband."

"And they were right," thought Anna. "How good our union has been and how fine a man Galen has become. The Counsellors need not have feared, and it is that old fear alone which touches me tonight."

She closed her eyes for a moment, emptying her mind of unsought and intrusive feelings as she had been taught to do as a child at school. She sensed his presence as she sat in the blindness of her fallen lids. When she opened her eyes a shadow loomed above her on the wall opposite her chair. Shrunk beneath it stood Galen watching her intently.

"I have been with my grandmother, but I am home now." His gaze slipped away from her to the stars high above them outside the window. She found that she was praying and that he, kneeling suddenly by her side, was grateful for her prayers.

# Chapter 3

Galen opened the front door quietly and stepped into the rich air of the morning, closely followed by Rachel and Nathan, their eyes alight with excitement. Above them, dawn streamed across the sky, bringing with it pools of light, faint bars of star-filtered mauve, whilst before them the buildings lay silhouetted in twilight.

Galen and the children walked along the empty paths, past the Centre of Worship, the sanctuary, the school buildings, and headed towards the meadows which lay beyond the edge of the last houses. They carried packs upon their backs, for inside was bread and honey that they would eat later for refreshment. Rachel took her father's hand whilst Nathan walked behind gazing ahead to the emerging landscape.

"How long will it take us, Father?" The expectancy in the boy's voice echoed Galen's own, even though they both knew the distance they had to travel.

"No more than an hour, my son. We shall arrive with the full light of morning."

How many times had he walked this way on his journey to the plain. He had first come with his grandfather, carried upon the older man's shoulders for much of the way, but that was long ago. Since then he had covered the same route whenever the opportunity arose, but the sight of the River and the Tree always made him gasp in wonder.

The buildings soon fell behind them, gradually disappearing from sight as they crossed the meadows and climbed up towards the woods. The dawn had made no impression amongst the foliage as yet, but they were sure-footed and took the short path unerringly through the trees. When they came out into the fields their pace quickened.

The crops stirred slightly as Galen and the children skirted the edge of the cultivated land, until they reached a clearly visible way which stretched ahead across rolling grassland.

"Can you smell the water?" Galen raised his head, breathing deeply, and the children followed his example. It was there, palpable in the air, a shaft of cold, an ice haze, a scent of frosty water.

They could see the sun rising now, bursting through the colours of night. Rachel danced up and down holding out her arms to the east, whilst Nathan stood immobile, his eyes reflecting the golden fire before him.

"Come." Galen's voice was husky in his desire not to break the splendour of the moment. They walked together towards the sun, on and on across the grasslands, until they dropped down the side of a hill into a narrow valley edged on either side with willowy trees. They were almost running now, following the descent to the plain below.

"When we turn the next corner we shall see!" cried Galen, and they ran with increased urgency. As they turned the bend their steps slackened until they stood looking down across the plain.

The River sparkled before them, catching the sunlight on its surface, drawing them forward with its music. In the far distance, across the other side of the plain, soared the mountains, glaciers glinting upon their breasts. They could not see where the water leapt into life, but the River flowed from beneath the mountains and across the plain, mighty in its crystal width.

There were no trees to obscure their view across the plain, though many flowers grew amongst the grasses. No trees except one, the Tree they had come to see, the one which all their people remembered as they went about their daily tasks. It soared out of the centre of the plain; its vast trunk was dark, but through its branches the light wove a pattern of silver and gold. The plain was gigantic, but the Tree towered over it, flattening it further so that the eye followed the line of the trunk up to the boughs overhead. The arms of the tree were held so wide that it seemed as if a multitude could shelter beneath their shade, and from the branches hung the fruit, gleaming in ruby clusters.

"The Tree," whispered the children, stepping closer to their father as they gazed with awe at such majesty.

"The Tree." His words mingled with their voices and it was a long time before anyone spoke again. At last Galen tore his eyes away from the sight before them.

"Come, we will walk across to the great River and there we will have our refreshment and rest."

"And then will you tell us the story, Father?" Rachel tugged at her father's hand. Galen laughed, filled suddenly with a great joy that urged him faster towards the water.

"Then I will tell you the story."

They had eaten sitting on the grasses near the edge of the River. It had been a silent meal. The sound of the water had seemed ample communion and the beauty of the Tree filled their minds so that their words were lost in thought but, now that the meal was finished, the children turned expectantly to their father. He began, telling the ancient tale in hushed tones, conscious of the time upon time it had been told before, aware that the recounting of it was part of the essential pattern of the lives of his people.

*In the beginning, before our people lived here, this land lay waiting like a golden cradle and, when we first walked upon it, we knew then, as we do now, where we came from. Whenever the people lifted their eyes they saw the light, whether the sky was filled with sunshine or the scudding clouds before the rain, or the nightly visit of the stars. After a while we multiplied and, as we increased in number, so our knowledge grew. Yet we always understood that our knowledge does not really belong to us; we use it only to help each other. In a way we are clothed in the lightness of our knowledge and that is why our people always dress as they do.*

*Now at the very beginning of our days, soon after the first Counsellors had been chosen, something happened that showed us once and for all how we must live our lives if we are to remain in this land. It happened like this.*

*Early one morning Jedra, one of the very first Counsellors, was walking on his own. He had left the people sleeping and slipped away as the sun started to rise. He wished to think and he felt that the morning beauty would help mould his thoughts. He had been walking for some time when he realised that he had no idea where he was. Indeed, he had been so deep in thought he had forgotten about the glory of the morning. He stood waiting for his sense of direction to lead him back to the people.*

*Suddenly he was aware of something approaching. It was not a noise which alerted him, for there was no sound except the gentle stirring of the wind. Rather it was a sense of some kind of life moving towards him like a...*

Galen paused, searching for the word, although he knew the old story so well. The children gazed at him, hardly breathing.

*...like a shadow.*

*Now children, in our land we understand many things and, most of all, we understand that we must always treasure the way we live. But we also know that there are things we must not search to find out and that, even here, there is a force*

15

that might try to drive us towards the false idea that we do not know enough. It is something we hardly comprehend. We know though that we must not seek to discover more than is safe for our people. That means that we can never think only of ourselves, for that may lead us away from all that we hold dear. You are being taught about this at school. It is partly because of that dawn walk of Jedra's that you learn such things.

On this morning Jedra stood staring into the distance. He found he was standing in a narrow valley, a valley embraced by slender trees, and now that he had stopped walking he felt suddenly cold and wished he had brought his cloak. For a moment he thought he must have been imagining things, but the sense of another presence grew stronger than ever, and it was then he saw coming towards him a creature he had never encountered before.

It stood taller than Jedra, yet it was no broader than one of his arms, and its whole body seemed of equal thickness. It had no legs, yet even as he gazed it drew closer. He could not be sure how it moved, but it appeared to glide upon its tail. Its skin was glossy reds and greens, beautiful in its rich colours, yet it did not attract him. Normally he would touch an animal in greeting, but on this occasion he unconsciously stepped back a little. The creature's eyes were small, unblinking, set back in a head that was merely an extension of its long body, and they looked into the eyes of Jedra with a kind of familiarity that made the Counsellor tremble. The eyes seemed to dart into his mind and the mouth was strangely mobile, revealing a tongue that struck into the air with a rapidity that was in vivid contrast to the measured rhythm of its motion.

The creature was now standing directly before Jedra. The breeze had dropped so that the only sound was that of the Counsellor's breathing. Instinctively he knew that the animal wished to lead him somewhere and that he must follow.

It swayed before him, floating over the valley floor, its tail brushing the grasses as it moved. Jedra walked behind, his eyes fixed on that slim body. Every now and then it turned and gazed back, checking the Counsellor's constancy, looking into his eyes with unblinking concentration. At last, after what seemed a circuitous and protracted journey, they came to the edge of a gigantic plain, and across the centre of the plain there flowed a great River and in the middle of the plain, close by the River, a mighty Tree towered, dazzling in its splendour.

Jedra fell upon his knees before such a magnificent sight, for the Tree shed a constant light, even whilst its branches were deep green and its massive trunk a rich, earth brown.

'What is this?' he whispered. He felt a light touch upon his cheek, the touch of dry, hard skin, and the swift caress of a tongue. The creature was bending over him, urging him by the rhythm of its body to follow further, even to the very base of the Tree. Jedra was afraid to go forward, yet he found himself obeying. Rising from his knees he followed the strange animal across the plain towards the Tree, the Tree that seemed to grow ever higher and more radiant as he approached.

Even as Jedra reached the first shade of the branches, the creature began to slide up the bark and, watching its movement, Jedra saw for the first time the fruit hanging beneath the boughs. He had never seen a fruit like it before, even though his people ate an abundance of different fruits. As he gazed in wonder there was a slight rustling sound and a moment later a crimson ball shone upon the ground at Jedra's feet.

'Eat!' The words were in the air, inside his mind, and the animal stood beside him again, its head higher than the

Counsellor's, its glistening body close to his flesh. 'Eat and know,' breathed the air, and the fruit lay at Jedra's feet, smooth and pure.

Jedra fell to his knees again, clasping his hands together, closing his eyes so that he could see clearly, and he saw the Tree grow even mightier, radiating a light that no man could look upon for long. On the ground in the dusty soil beneath the Tree lay the creature, now full length upon its belly, its eyes staring out of its small head, its tongue swollen and hanging from its mouth. And on the ground lay the fruit, with jagged teeth marks upon it where a large piece of its flesh had been removed, and it was bruised and rotting even as he stared in horror.

Tears ran down Jedra's cheeks for he understood at once that, if he ate it, the knowledge that followed would destroy him and his people. And at first he was not sure whether it was he who had bitten into the fruit that decayed at his feet. He ran his tongue around his mouth. It was clean. No traces of fruit were there; he had not eaten.

And the creature? Disappeared, gone as if it had never been, and where the fruit had lain only grasses glimmered with the dew.

Jedra returned to his people and summoned them to a special gathering. He told them what had happened and held before them a drawing he had made of the creature. The people gazed in silence at the picture, burning its image into their hearts as a warning that the Tree can be sheltered beneath, but to eat its fruit would be to open the way to the knowledge that would destroy them.

On that day, in the early beginning, Jedra looked on the silent people for a long time after he had told them his story. Then he held wide his arms and cried loudly:

'Awe Praise Prayer Light Eternal

*Adoration Peace People Love Enduring*
*Acceptance Promise Practice Life Everlasting.'*

*And the multitude took up the chanting, repeating the words*
*again and again, until the whole place seemed filled with*
*the music of their meaning. And that is how the fruit upon*
*the Tree came to be called an apple, and that is why we*
*always begin our worship with the words handed down to*
*us by Jedra.*

When Galen had finished speaking he jumped up abruptly
and stood staring at the Tree. The children watched him
without saying anything. They had heard the story several
times before, but each telling captured their imaginations as
if it were the first narration.

The morning light seemed to pinpoint the fruit hanging
from the boughs. As they gazed upwards a slight trembling
amongst some of the lower branches made them draw
closer together; there was no wind and the leaves had
been motionless until now. They waited breathlessly. The
apple fell softly to the ground and lay at their feet in mute
perfection. Nathan and Rachel gasped, taking their father's
hands in consternation.

"It is like the story," whispered Nathan in awe, "except
there is no creature and no voice tells us to eat."

Of one accord they knelt together, still clasping hands,
closing their eyes against the brilliant light.

Rachel's voice shook slightly. "What shall we do, Father?"

It was Nathan who answered. "Wait a few moments and
then we may open our eyes." The boy felt his father's nails
digging into his hands and was about to speak again when
Rachel jumped to her feet.

"The apple has gone!" Nathan felt a stirring round his
heart and looked on the ground. Only grasses covered the

place where the apple had lain.

Galen stood up slowly and tried to smile.

"Time to set off back home if we are to go to the food gathering before Early Worship." Rachel stayed close to her father as he collected up the packs, shrugging his own onto his back, tossing them each their bundle, but Nathan stood at a little distance and his young face was solemn and pale. "Run on ahead, I will catch you up in just a moment."

Nathan hesitated.

"Come with us, Father, do not stay alone under the Tree."

"Go!" Galen's voice was louder than he intended and, seeing the startled looks of his children, he softened his tone. "I will be with you in a moment."

Reluctantly they turned to leave him, but they did not hurry. Nathan took his sister's hand and squeezed it, trying to reassure her that all was as it should be, and she smiled at him gratefully. Galen remained watching the Tree intently through half-closed eyes. Sunlight played on the branches and the fruit hung succulently beneath the boughs. He ran his tongue over his lips, dampening the dry skin. His blond hair shone in the light whilst his eyes glowed deeper than ever and, in his absorbedness, he was not aware of the moments passing.

"Father, Father!" The children had sensed that he was not following them and had turned to summon him, but the sight of his still back subdued their shouts. Nathan felt a sudden stab of pain in his head, startling because pain was virtually unknown to him. He knew he must call out again and break the silence.

"Father!" There was an urgency to the child's voice that stirred Galen from his reverie and he turned.

"Nathan, Nathan my son, I am coming, wait for me."

In a few strides he was with them, and in the chatter of the homeward journey Galen forgot their momentary separation, but Nathan could not erase the memory of the apple lying on the ground, and the touch of his father's nails as they dug into his flesh.

# Chapter 4

It was still early morning as Galen and the children made their way across the plain, up the sloping valley, over grasslands and past rich crops to the woodland path. Light glimpsed between the trees now and, as they came out into the meadows, they could see the contours of the Centre of Worship silhouetted against the sky.

"We will make our way straight to the food gathering," said Galen, "and then take the produce to mother before we go to the Celebration of Awakening."

As they drew nearer they could see people emerging from the houses heading towards the cluster of low, warmly timbered buildings that lay on the edge of the dwellings, and could hear the voices of greeting ringing through the air. Rachel ran ahead of her father and brother, catching up with the flow of walkers, slipping her hand into that of one of the Counsellors.

The tables were laid out ready, piled steeply with food: fresh baked bread, wooden bowls of jam, great urns of frothing milk, fruit filling the wicker baskets in an abundance of colour. Behind the first rows of tables lay the stores for the evening meal: vegetables of many kinds, cheeses, bunches of herbs from the garden of the elders. The people moved in steady rhythm, taking what food they needed, discussing their selection with each other, sniffing appreciatively at the aroma of warm bread, wishing each other a refreshing breakfast.

By the time Galen caught up with his young daughter she had chosen a loaf of bread and was thoughtfully contemplating a basket of fruit, her hand hovering over some ripe peaches.

"Now Rachel, you have already had one breakfast." Galen smiled, nodding in mutual salutation to the Counsellor standing next to her, to neighbours and fellow workers, to old school fellows and many more.

"But that was a long time ago and I will be hungry when we return from the Celebration, before I go to school."

"Quite right, my daughter." The Counsellor smiled over the child's head at Galen. It was Hedron, one of the oldest male Counsellors and a particular friend to Galen and Anna. "And where have you been so early on this beautiful morning?"

For a moment Galen hesitated. "We have been to the great River and to the Tree."

"And Father told us the ancient story," burst out Nathan.

"Oh yes." Hedron was studying Galen's face intently, his kind eyes filled with watchful love, although his words were addressed to the child. "And what do you understand by the story your father told you?"

"I understand that the fruit of the Tree must never be eaten. We can never know its taste. If we tried to taste an apple we cannot begin to understand where that might lead us. We might sometimes think we would like to know. I have never felt like that, but I could imagine..."

"Imagine?"

"It would be as if something had stepped into your mind; if you do not listen, if you stay quite still, that presence will go."

"How do you know such things so young?" murmured Hedron, but he did not look for an answer. Instead he turned again to Galen, putting his hand on the younger man's shoulder. "Perhaps, Galen, it is best to visit the Tree in the company of other adults; it is a great responsibility to go alone with the children. Such a pilgrimage is always a time of wonder, but a state of wonder must always be disciplined."

"You are right, Hedron; my keenness to share the experience with the children made me hasty. In future I shall seek the balance of wiser minds."

The Counsellor hesitated before he spoke again.

"That is good. I will see you a little later at the Celebration of Awakening." He drew back, lightly spreading his palms over the heads of the children, and Galen nodded, grateful the conversation was ended.

"Come, you two, we have sufficient food for our day's needs." Rachel ran to her father holding out the basket of food; there was just enough for their requirements, no more. At his side Nathan held the jug of milk. They were ready to return to Anna.

The tables were almost empty now as the people started to make their way back to the dwellings. Only Hedron remained motionless by the timber huts. His lips moved soundlessly and his eyes were fixed upon the morning sky. He stood there long after Galen and the children had disappeared from sight and, when finally he stirred, his steps were slower than usual and the faintest trace of a line could be seen upon his forehead.

Anna was waiting at the door, her arms held out in welcome.

"Why, how happy I am to see you!" She met each pair of eyes with her own laughing warmth, pressing her cheeks against their faces, exchanging kisses upon each forehead. Rachel could hardly contain herself.

"Mother, Mother, we have been on such a journey *and* we have been to the food gathering." Anna held the child close.

"So I see, but come, we must leave at once. Afterwards, you can tell me your story." Over the head of the little girl she sought the eyes of her husband. His blond hair hung around his face, almost as white as his garments in the bright sunshine. He was not looking at her but was gazing into the distance.

"What do you see, Galen?" Nathan went and slipped an arm through his mother's whilst they waited for the answer.

"I see again the Tree in all its glory, and I know that I must not eat of its fruit."

The people entered the Centre of Worship as with a single heartbeat. The Counsellors stood close by the ancient table with outstretched arms ready to lead the Celebration. Men and women, young and old, babes in arms, poured into the lofty building and still more came until the whole place was filled. Galen and Anna stood with the children, their voices merging with the others. The song was of the blessing of morning, the beauty of the land, the love of family and friends, the contentment of work and the joy of learning.

When the singing was over and the hush of prayers still held the air with its concentration, one of the Counsellors made a sign to the people that he wished to speak. It was Hedron.

"Dear friends, I know that it is unusual for any of us to address you during the Celebration of Awakening, but I must speak to you now to remind us all for a moment about the way we live and share our lives.

"We all believe that, whatever talents we have been blessed with, each one of us is essential to the pattern and harmony of our land. We also know that the Tree is a manifestation of the light and the sight of it fills us with awe and the memory of it guides all our days. We cannot see its roots or follow its branches into the sky, but we may shelter beneath its arms. We know that the fruit of the Tree is sacred, found nowhere else in our land and that we may not touch it. We understand that there are some things we can never know, some knowledge we must never seek. Let us be certain that, whenever we approach the Tree, we are prepared for the sight of its glory."

There was a murmur of agreement amongst the people and Hedron held his arms wide above him as a signal for the final song to begin. Nathan sang with the congregation, but he glanced up to his father with a questioning look. Galen, his head flung back, was singing as intently as everyone else, but the boy's voice trembled as the music soared all around him.

Breakfast was finished and Nathan and Rachel had left for school. Galen too was ready for his day's work. Anna was not due at the sanctuary until later in the morning and she was tidying up after the family meal.

"Nathan was very quiet at breakfast." The statement was lightly spoken, but Galen's voice sought reassurance.

"Indeed. The children were affected by their journey to the Tree, especially Nathan. I do not think you should take them on your own again, Galen."

"You are right." For a moment, Galen hesitated. "It is not often a Counsellor speaks at the Celebration of Awakening; I wonder why Hedron did so today?" Anna took her husband's hands, holding them briefly to her face.

"No, Galen, but it was a reminder that we must always treat the fruit of the Tree as untouchable." He nodded his assent, although he did not reply. His hands still lay in hers and Anna felt the fingers curl inwards towards the palms. His eyes were half closed as he rested his chin upon her silky head.

"The plain has never seemed as vast as it did this morning, and the Tree rose into the sky, holding the fruit in its arms like a precious gift."

"No, Galen! The fruit is not a gift but a reminder of how we may be fruitful. If we touch it we will know only how to destroy its growth, and ourselves!"

"Do you never long to see to the top of the Tree, Anna?" Galen was looking at his wife now, holding her face between his hands.

"Why no, never, that would be impossible! No eye could strain that far, or look into the brilliance that crowns the upper branches." He released her, turning towards the door with hesitant steps.

"You are right, Anna. I must be going or else my comrades will be looking for me."

"Galen!" She ran to him. "Wait. Tell me that this evening we will go together to see Hedron." The answer came too quickly.

"Not this evening. First I must visit my grandmother."

"Again?" She had not meant the words to come so rapidly.

"When the moment is right we will talk with Hedron."

By the time Anna had formed the words to say that their visit must take precedence, he had gone. She felt an unaccustomed heaviness of spirit. It was foolish of her to try and discuss something so important when he had just returned from the Tree. She must be patient.

She moved around the house swiftly, attempting to empty her mind, to focus on what there was to do, but it was no good. Although she did not look outside, she knew that the sun shone brighter than ever and that on the plain the River surged beneath its piercing light, whilst the fruit upon the Tree hung succulent and shining amongst its branches.

# Chapter 5

Anna had been working in the sanctuary for several hours. It was mid-afternoon and a sleepy tranquility enveloped the building. Young and old drowsed, either in airy rooms with windows wide open to the breeze, or in the garden where the trees dappled sunlight onto the grass.

The old slept lightly, drifting in and out of consciousness. They lay upon couches in their white garments facing the sky, so that when they opened their eyes they could see the light through the branches, or else glancing in through the lofty windows. The babies slept deeply, wrapped in white shawls, resting snugly in cribs made at the wood-turning centre. The mothers slumbered also, lying upon fleecy rugs on the grass. Anna usually loved this time of day when she walked with the other helpers from quiet room to quiet room, across the garden, checking that no-one needed a gentle touch or murmured word, but today the smallest shadow lay across her heart. She thought frequently of Galen in the forest, praying that he was at one with his work and his comrades, enjoying the rhythm of shared labour.

Sounds of life could be heard as the sleepers stirred. For the most part the old ones would not leave their couches, preserving what little strength they had left to prepare themselves for the final journey. The helpers always knew when an old one was leaving, for the family would arrive whatever time of day or night.

Now, as Anna walked in the garden carrying bowls of pungent smelling refreshment, she wondered how long it would be until Galen's grandmother asked to be brought to the sanctuary so that she could share her journey with fellow travellers. Galen's grandfather had left the year before, but his grandmother remained, patiently biding her time.

"Anna." It was Heccra calling, one of the female Counsellors, greatly respected for her wisdom. She lay on the couch, her white hair spread over the pillows. Anna was with her in an instant, kneeling by her side so that they could exchange the greeting of love.

"My family will be here in a few moments, Anna." The old lady's lips moved slowly as the words melted into the younger woman's ear. "I wish to say a last word to you, my child, and please hear it as it is uttered, with an open heart." Anna stirred upon her knees, taking the Counsellor's hand and holding it briefly against her cheek.

"I am listening."

"Then, Anna, use your special qualities of sympathy to watch over Galen." Anna started, drawing back for a moment before leaning closer.

"Galen? Why, Heccra, I do. What are you saying?"

"As I go on the final journey, I feel the need to speak. Galen has such beauty of spirit. All our people are bathed in light, but none with such strength of brightness as your husband. We are united in the way we live but sometimes I wonder if Galen feels in some way different from the rest of our people?"

"Different?" The word hung in the air between them like a lost sigh. Heccra drew her closer.

"You know him best. If you have any doubt at all, turn to one of the other Counsellors; we all have to be vigilant, whilst at the same time having unclouded trust. We must never seek knowledge that is beyond our understanding, Anna."

The old lady closed her eyes. Across the grass Anna could see Heccra's family approaching: small children, young men and women, those of middle years and the more elderly, bringing the gift of their releasing love. Anna kissed Heccra upon the forehead.

"Goodbye."

"Come, Anna, and join us for a while," called a young mother who sat feeding her baby and talking with some of the other young women. Anna walked slowly towards the group. She took one of the babies into her arms, holding it close against her, and rocked the child gently.

When she went back inside all was peaceful and she sat down with some of the other helpers as they sipped the steaming liquid and chatted whilst they rested for a few moments.

"No-one has been in with anything special today." It was Maius speaking, a near neighbour of Anna's, a fine poet of the people, as well as a teacher at the school. He helped at the sanctuary one afternoon a week.

"Well, none of the children have over-exerted themselves in the games, nor any adults forgotten their concentration as they go about their tasks," smiled one of the doctors.

Anna looked around at the group of contented faces. The sanctuary was always a very special place to be, with the arrival of new babies or the quiet departing of one of the old. Occasionally others came; children who had hurt themselves slightly, the more mature who had been lost in a task and injured themselves a little. The doctors always dealt with such instances swiftly, the bones quickly knitting, the skin rapidly renewing. It was rare for anyone to be detained for longer than an hour or two unless they were very old or waiting for the birth of a child. Healing took place almost spontaneously for any hurts.

"Except," thought Anna as the memory flooded into her head with unexpected force, "except that time when Galen tore his hands so badly."

A small boy stood in the doorway, his eyes filled with

30

moisture although he was smiling.

"Heccra has left us; will you join us for the final Song of Departing?"

Nathan sat with his school fellows listening to the words of the Counsellor. Across the floor of the spacious hall the young people formed a united aura of concentration. Whatever their age, this hour, when one of the Counsellors came to talk to the children, was regarded as the culmination of the day's learning. Nathan was usually sorry when the school day ended for he loved to study, but today a shadow lay across his heart.

The Counsellor had finished speaking and the school day was ended but, long after the other students had left the hall, Nathan remained motionless, gazing out of the window yet seeing nothing. Rachel had waited for him to go home with her, holding out her hand so they could walk together as usual, but for once he remained behind.

"Tell mother I will be home soon." She left him reluctantly, glancing back to make sure he had not changed his mind.

"At what do you stare with such seriousness, Nathan?" The boy had not heard the approach of the Counsellor and started slightly.

"I see nothing." Nathan turned to smile at his questioner.

"Nothing? And in your head?" Hedron prompted gently.

"I saw my father standing by the mighty Tree and felt…" The boy paused, struggling to describe his emotion.

"Fear?" The quiet voice of the Counsellor seemed to echo round the hall.

"Is that what I feel? Fear? Why, I thought…"

"You thought?"

"Only if I ate an apple and I never…"

"The fear that will pull you into darkness will only come if you eat of the fruit. Your fear is not for yourself, Nathan."

"So why…?"

"Only a few of us see the road to the way of darkness. We are sent as guardians of our people. We work with the people that we may all live under the branches of the Tree, but never seek to eat its fruit."

"Then I will be…?"

"That is not to think of now, Nathan."

"And my father?"

"Ah, your father has many of the qualities of a Counsellor but – there is also something that sets him a little apart – makes him too – individual – for such a role." Hedron paused, looking keenly at the boy, wondering how much he understood.

"I understand. Amongst all the spirits of our people, my father's shines the brightest. Everyone feels it. Yet he is the only one amongst the people who makes you notice him…. apart." The word was said again, hovering between them in the sunlit afternoon. Hedron nodded; the boy had a wisdom far beyond his years.

"You understand well."

The boy shivered, although it was warm in the hall.

"Oh I pray I will be like you and help to join the spirit of my father with the rhythm of this land."

"Keep quiet watch, my child, and come to me or any of the Counsellors if you feel there is a need to do so."

"And my mother?"

"Ah, your mother has a special heart."

"Yes, she does, she does! She will always guard him with her love."

Hedron did not reply. Bending swiftly he exchanged the greeting of mutual warmth and care with the boy and, feeling much comforted, Nathan left the hall and soon could be seen running across the lawn to where his sister still stood waiting.

# Chapter 6

Although dusk hung in the air its shadows as yet were formless, and the warm breeze stirred with the scent of flowers. The family had eaten outside, sharing the food they had collected earlier in the day. Now the meal was over the children roamed around the garden, the older amongst them linking hands with the little ones, whilst their elders put into focus and perspective the patterns of their day.

Only Galen's grandmother rested a little apart, lying on the couch that had been carefully placed so she could gaze at the flowers as they melted into the twilight. The talk of crops and craftsmanship, of the work of the doctors and Counsellors, of the latest writings amongst the people, eddied round her like the whisperings of distant waters.

Anna had been watching the old lady for some time, and now she slipped away from the group and glided across the lawn to where she lay. The grandmother never turned her head or looked away from the sky, but she knew Anna had come and she understood at once that these had been no ordinary steps across the grass.

"See, Anna, though the sky is beginning to darken, the colours do not disappear, they merely become more profound."

Anna knelt by the old lady and rested her face against the white hand that lay motionless on the couch.

"Grandmother, may I speak to you about Galen?" Now the ancient eyes were turned to look into the face of the younger woman.

"What you wish to know I hardly know myself."

"Why does no-one ever speak of how Galen came to receive the scars upon his hands? Nobody else carries such marks, yet when I have questioned him he says it was just an abundance of boyish energy, that it happened so long ago the memory has vanished."

"Ah, is that what he says?" The old lady took the smooth face into her cupped palms. "And you?"

"There is something different in Galen. His beauty sets him apart, yet there is something that…" The words trailed off, lost in the air.

The old lady was silent for a few moments and Anna began to wonder if she had fallen asleep. At first she was hardly aware of the voice that whispered to her out of the increasing darkness, for the words seemed to come from the evening breeze.

*From the beginning there was something about Galen that set him a little apart from our people. When he was born his beauty was remarkable, as it is still, but it was the beauty of his spirit that made even the Counsellors wonder at its source. All our people work and live in harmony, understanding and following the teachings that have been given to us, but Galen seemed to understand everything long before he went to school, before his parents, his teachers or any of the Counsellors had spoken to him of the great River and the mighty Tree and the creature that came at the beginning and has not been seen since.*

*How did he know these things? Do not ask me, for many a wiser person than I has pondered this question. But his understanding only enhanced his beauty and, as he grew through those early years, the love he radiated touched everyone. We all thought he was marked to be a Counsellor, a Counsellor as fine as Jedra who is remembered above all the other Counsellors. At least we did until the accident. After that Galen seemed content to take a quieter role, eventually joining the forest workers when he left school, although he was a scholar at heart.*

Anna stirred. All this she knew already. She had grown up with Galen and, like the other children, had responded to the presence of his spirit and his beauty again and again.

"But that day, Grandmother, the day of the accident…?"

"I will tell you. Allow me time to gather my thoughts."

Anna felt the reluctance of the older woman as she approached the heart of her narrative, and said no more.

*It was Galen's tenth birthday and the day was a Holy Day. For some time he had been asking me to take him across the plain to the mountains on the other side. The two of us had often walked to the foot of the Tree with some of our people, for Galen loved to see the River and the Tree and he never grew tired of hearing the ancient story. Unlike the rest of our people, however, who wished to go no further, whenever Galen stood on the plain, his gaze was frequently drawn to those far mountains and the glaciers that glinted upon them.*

*'Oh let us go, Grandmother,' he would whisper, his eyes sparkling like the glaciers themselves and, I must admit, I longed to take him, for the glory of the hills cried out to me also and I yearned to get closer. As a girl I had once gone to the far edge of the plain with some school fellows and two of the Counsellors, but there had been no question of venturing further. However, the sight that day of the mountains towering ahead of us made an indelible impression upon me, so that I would wake up with the image of the peaks filling my mind.*

*On that particular day we went to the Celebration of Awakening as usual. The rain had been falling but, when we emerged from the Centre of Worship, the sun had broken out and the world smelt of evaporating raindrops. As it was a special day, several of our people walked with us to the plain, but only Galen and I were to go forward. I had told our companions that I wished to take the boy to the far edge and, although one or two of them had suggested we ask a Counsellor to go with us, such an excursion was not unheard of. I did not mention the thought that we might venture into the foothills and so get closer to the mountains. How often since have I asked myself how I contemplated such a thing.*

*You know the walk to the River and the Tree. That day the special glory of the morning silenced conversation as our group travelled together.*

*I do not remember how many we were; perhaps ten or fifteen. I do remember that one of the Counsellors was with us and he was the second to arrive at the foot of the Tree. Galen was there before anyone and he was already gazing up in wonder as we approached.*

*How excited Galen was that morning. Everyone smiled to see his delight. He could hardly contain himself as we all knelt by the Tree. It was at its most glorious that morning, the fruit glistening beneath the branches. As we knelt, there was a rustling above us in the branches although there was no wind, and an apple dropped to the ground. It shocked us all for this had never happened before, but most of all it startled Galen. Perhaps that was because it fell near his feet. He cried aloud and held out his hand.*

*'Oh see my people!'*

*The Counsellor was kneeling beside Galen and, when the child cried out, he took his hand and held it tightly.*

*'Do not touch the fruit, Galen; it is holy and not for human hands.'*

*We gazed at Galen, for his beauty at that moment seemed to surpass anything we had seen before. He looked up at the Counsellor and his cheeks were flushed red like the skin of the apple that lay near his feet.*

*'I was not going to touch the fruit. I was startled for a moment.'*

*'My sister.' It was Hedron who had walked with us that morning. He was a young Counsellor then. 'Do you think perhaps you should delay your journey across the plain? We do not understand why the apple has fallen.'*

*'I have promised Galen, Father, and it is his birthday. The apple remains untouched. It must be a good sign that it has fallen today. We shall be back long before the Evening Worship,' and with that Hedron had to be content, for he had no reason to forbid us and he trusted me completely with the child. Briefly he pressed my forehead with his hand.*

*'Go then in quietness of spirit, seeking only that which it is right to know.'*

*We had exchanged farewells with our people and walked a few yards away from them when a loud exclamation made us turn around. Beneath the Tree the grasses were dotted here and there with tiny flowers but, where the apple had lain, the sunlight fell upon empty ground.*

Anna gazed at the grandmother's face, but she did not speak.

"The apple had gone, Anna, and the spirit of Galen shone more brightly than ever. What happened seemed a good sign. We all felt it."

Anna tried to smile, inclining her head and, after a short silence, the whispered voice of the old lady filled the night air again.

*We talked happily together as we walked. At least we did until we drew close to the far side. We fell silent then. We both knew that we would go further. When we reached the extremity of the plateau we joined hands and turned to gaze at the Tree. It looked a long way away. For a moment I hesitated; we could have a little refreshment and then retrace our steps. I opened my mouth to tell Galen that we would go no further but, before I could speak, the distant sound of cracking ice caught our attention and we turned to stare up at the mountains.*

*'Grandmother,' he called repeatedly, holding out his arms, 'look at the way up to the peaks where the light grows even more brilliant.'*

*I smiled at his rapture, sharing it in part. He looked all light himself at that moment, his white-gold curls falling around his face. In that final second I hesitated for the last time; it was not too late to change our minds. I turned once more to look at the Tree in the far distance and a sudden longing swept over me to take Galen by the hand and run across the flat grasses to the shelter of its arms. But Galen, in his excitement, saw nothing but the way to the mountains and I could not bear to disappoint him.*

"Oh why did you not stop him – he was only a child!"

The old lady trembled.

"Do not ask me, Anna, I beg you."

"And so you did not...?"

*And so we left the plain and began to climb up towards the glaciers. The sun shone with greater brilliance than ever and the roar of the water emerging from the ice sounded like voices we had never heard before. I could not tell you how long we climbed, but to me it seemed an arduous ascent. After some time Galen grew very tired and so we found shelter from the sun by the side of some rocks, and there we ate our bread and drank the freezing water from a nearby stream.*

*I must have fallen asleep; I do not know why for I had never before slept during the day. Perhaps the sound of water and*

38

the heat of the afternoon lulled me into unconsciousness. How long I slept I could not say, but I awoke to the knowledge that Galen was no longer with me. I knew immediately that he had not just wandered a few paces from our shady spot; I felt the determination of his absence and some instinct told me that he had been drawn away. It was a little cooler now and mist hung over the glaciers. We should be starting the return journey.

For a while I searched nearby, but he was not there. At last I stilled myself and held out my arms and waited; only then did I know which way I must go.

I found him. I have told you that by now the mist had brought a chill to the air. I pulled my cloak around my shoulders and began to climb. I saw him lying on the ground, still as one of the rocks on which he lay. His eyes were closed and there were a few scratches on his face. But it was the sight of his hands that made me cry aloud in consternation. They were torn and bleeding with holes in the flesh like gaping eyes, and the blood ran from the wounds to the ground and blackened it. I ran to his side and knelt beside him, cradled his head in my arms, lifted his poor hands so that the blood ran over my own flesh.

'Galen, Galen!' I cried. And as I knelt there I sensed the presence of something else in that deserted place. In my concern for Galen I did not look around, but I thought I heard a rustling sound, as if a light object had brushed over fallen leaves. As the noise faded Galen opened his eyes. What I saw there, Anna, I had never before witnessed, nor have I seen it since.

When Galen spoke at last, his words were confused and breathless.

'A wall, Grandmother, barring the way, had to try to climb it, difficult, difficult, tore my hands on the sharp stones, at the top, noises, never heard, sounds...a boy, like me only *different, I knew him, I called, noises louder, must have fallen, fallen...'*

*I carried him all the way back home. I do not know how I found the strength. I remember nothing of the journey except the need to return to our people, to take Galen to the sanctuary so that he could be healed.*

*The doctors could not understand the wounds and they were very concerned. They questioned me again and again but I could not tell them about the words Galen had spoken in his bewilderment. As for Galen, he remembered nothing, and I thought the best thing was to return to the rhythm of our lives. But the wounds did not heal as usual and he stayed in the sanctuary a long time. You know that such a prolonged stay is unheard of amongst our people. The doctors tried all their skills and the Counsellors came also.*

"Yet you did not tell them everything?"

"You know, Anna, that the only words to be heard are those that are freely told."

"But if they are held back?" Anna found it difficult to breathe, for the story had troubled her beyond imagining.

"Then perhaps, after all, words will not suffice."

"Perhaps then," – Anna found herself trembling – "perhaps then the time for words is past."

For a while the two women were silent. It was grandmother who spoke first, although she had closed her eyes with exhaustion.

"Something is coming to us across the grass."

Anna did not turn but she saw the shadow fall beside her. It was Galen.

His hair gleamed, falling around the beautiful mobility of his face as he smiled down at the two women with loving grace.

"It is almost time to leave for Worship." His voice was tender as he helped Anna to her feet and bent swiftly to exchange the signs of love with his grandmother. "Come Grandmother, I will carry you into the house before we go so that you do not become cold in the evening air."

She held out her arms to him like a child and Galen gathered her close, taking her to each member of the family in turn so that she could bid them goodnight. The old ones could usually walk until they started the final journey, but Galen's grandmother was overcome with a tiredness deep in her body and now she rarely took more than a few steps. Because of this she no longer attended the last Worship of the day although she was present at all the other gatherings. Galen took her into the house, to the light, airy bedroom on the ground floor where she slept. When he had settled her comfortably he paused for a moment as he bent to press his cheek against hers.

"Why did you tell Anna that story tonight?"

"You knew?"

He nodded briefly.

"She asked. She has never asked before."

"Ah, I see. But you do not know all the story, Grandmother."

"Why, Galen, I am aware of that. Ever since that day I have been silent, hoping the story was ended; lately I have known for certain that it was not. I thought if I spoke to Anna, then you would find the will to discover the words."

"If it is not the other way around." He knelt beside her and placed his head upon her lap as he had done as a child. With an unsteady hand she stroked the white curls.

"The time has come to visit one of the Counsellors, Galen. I should have encouraged you to go before, but at first I thought you remembered nothing. When I realised that was not so, I still persuaded myself that it was best to leave the past dormant. I thought my prayers would suffice; I did not listen to our teachings."

"Grandmother, do not talk like that. You have done everything out of love. I will speak to Anna later tonight after Worship and, if we think it necessary, I will go to one of the Counsellors. Rest quietly now, as all our land and its people rest at the end of each day and throughout our circling time."

They were seated by the window so that they could see the stars. The scent of evening drifted into the bedroom bringing with it the taste of dew. The children were sleeping.

Anna waited. They both knew that Galen would speak to her about that journey; there was no need for preliminaries, no desire for explanations. Hands linked, they wished only to share everything at last.

*Grandmother has told you all she remembers and all that she knows. She was right. I was startled when the apple fell by my feet that morning. I heard the rustling in the branches of the Tree; there was no wind but the leaves moved and the fruit landed next to my kneeling figure. How perfect it was, and how luscious in its perfection. For a second I wanted to take it in my hand, not to eat it – no – I would never have bitten into it, never – but to feel its smooth skin on my palm.*

*The words of Hedron checked me even as I stretched out my arm. For a few moments after that I felt uplifted, lighter than I had ever felt, as though my body hardly existed and I was a part of the air itself. I knew I must go on across the plain to the foot of the mountains and climb to the bottom of the nearest glacier. Oh, Anna, I was so young, only ten. When we reached the edge of the plain we paused to look back at the Tree and for a moment I felt an urge to run to the shelter of its branches, but the sound of cracking ice caught my attention and after that I had eyes for nothing but the unknown territory ahead. As we travelled towards the first glacier I was overwhelmed with joy for the way seemed all light. There was nothing grandmother could have done to stop me, nothing at all. After our meal she fell asleep. Perhaps she was tired after the walk, but it was the first time I had known her to sleep during the day. She was so strong at that time, indeed no woman of her age was stronger. As she lay resting I had a sudden urge to explore the way ahead on my own.*

*I do not know how long I walked but suddenly a huge shadow fell across my path. I was so startled I stumbled and for a few moments I dared not look up. At first I thought that the sun must have vanished, but it was not that. When at last I raised my eyes I cried aloud in astonishment. Above me reared a massive wall, a wall so high it was blocking out the sun.*

"A wall! There is no wall on the mountain side. Why, we would have heard about it."

"I saw a wall, Anna. Tall and terrible, it towered over me, built of rocks and stones. With a young boy's fascination I ran and placed my ear against base of the wall and heard… heard sounds that were not of this land."

"There is no other land!"

Galen shook his head, pressing Anna's hands urgently.

*The sounds called me. I do not wish to describe them, but my head felt as though it would burst open and I wanted to cry out aloud. Later I realised it had been fear I felt, but at that moment I seemed to move through events almost without understanding what was happening to me. The sounds were terrible, yet they called me. I had to try and climb the wall although the flesh on my hands tore as I did so and the pain was terrible. Somehow I found footholds, somehow I*

*pulled myself up. I do not know how long it took, but when
I reached the top I was gasping with effort and exhaustion.
I could hardly see…see…*

"What did you see, Galen?" Anna was staring at him with
frightened eyes.

*I saw sand, sand stretching on and on. But that is not what
amazed me. Climbing up the wall on the other side was a
boy about my age. He was looking at me as he ascended;
such beautiful, clear green eyes he had and tumbling black
curls.*

*I called to him: 'Boy! Boy! Who are you? Where are we?'*

*I did not hear his answer, but our eyes met and a great
yearning filled my heart. At that moment I must have lost
consciousness and fallen. When I opened my eyes again I
was lying in the arms of my grandmother.*

"And the wall?"

"The wall was nowhere to be seen."

"So you had imagined it!" Relief made Anna's voice
crack with emotion.

"There was a wall which only I could see. There is another
land that is bordered by empty sand. There is another people
that reach towards us."

"Why should only you know this, Galen?"

"That I cannot answer. For a long time after that day I
dreamt at night of the wall and especially of the boy whose
eyes I had looked into for a brief moment. But I told no-one,
even though the doctors and Counsellors asked me many
questions and sensed my withdrawal."

"But why did you tell no-one, why?" Anna struggled
to follow her husband's thoughts. "That denies the open
nature of our people and leads away from the lightness of

uncluttered thoughts."

"I cannot explain my silence, except to say that in some way I felt I could not speak of the boy I had met, that if I did I would," Galen paused for a moment, "harm him."

"How could such a possibility even enter your mind? Why, such a thing could never be! Our people live through their love of each other; how could one person harm another?"

Galen looked at his wife imploringly, his face taut with bewilderment.

"Do not ask me, but as a ten year old boy the sounds I heard through the wall made me think about the possibility of such harm."

"No wonder you seem a little apart from our people. For thirty years this thought has lodged within you."

"It was hardly there, Anna; it faded until I could almost think it was nothing at all. Recently, though, it has begun to return, and when I visited the Tree with Nathan and Rachel the memory flooded into my head in full force."

"I felt its presence," whispered Anna, "and I asked you again and again if you would open your heart to me. Now you have done so, I beg you to talk to one of the Counsellors."

"Before that I must go again across the plain and see if I can find the wall and the boy, so I can be sure that when I speak, my words will be the right ones."

"The boy will be a man now as you are. It was thirty years ago."

"I must find him." The grip of his hand was almost painful.

"Oh, Galen, you must not go alone." In her concern Anna rose to her feet and went to the open window. Outside the stars drew their patterns on the dark canvas of the sky.

"I will know him." She hardly recognised her husband's voice as he intoned the words to himself. "When I have met him again, I will come to the Counsellors and tell them everything. That is the way it must be."

Anna knew there was no more she could say and nothing she could do to make him change his mind. She drew the curtains against the night and turned to face him.

"When do you leave on your journey?"

"I go at first light. Will you help me prepare?"

With all her heart she longed to succour him.

"I will help you."

# Chapter 7

He had never before walked alone to the Tree. Since Jedra's solitary journey through that early dawning, it had been a sacred rule amongst their people that no less than two could make the pilgrimage, and the Tree bowed over its fruit and witnessed their quiet obedience. For the first time, Galen's action was breaking that shared understanding and acceptance.

He paused as he approached the Centre of Worship. Although dawn was still merely a whisper in the eastern sky, the glow above the building shone as at noon. He knew that inside some of the Counsellors would be watching through the night, for the building was never left unattended. He paused as he approached and some instinct made him hold out his hand towards the entrance even as his feet took him to the wide doors. He touched one briefly and caught his breath in surprise as it swung open.

Two Counsellors stood there, arms outstretched in worship. He wanted to join them but could not, for how could he begin to explain what he was doing. When he returned he would talk to the people and share with them all that had happened. Now he had only the beginning of the story; when he spoke he must have the end also. He turned away.

"Galen Nodeef."

Was it one of the Counsellors speaking or did the voice come from elsewhere? Wherever it came from he could not heed it. He must go forward and listen only to the words inside his own head which led him to the wall and the lost boy of his childhood. He turned to leave, the ritual greeting unsaid, and the door closed behind him.

Although they made no sign, the Counsellors knew Galen stood there. With all their strength they strove to draw him towards the ancient table and, as the door swung shut again on his retreating back, the effort of their endeavour left them momentarily weakened.

"Where is Galen going at this early hour, and alone?" It was the younger Counsellor who spoke and his voice contained an unusual urgency. "May I follow him and ask him to return here and worship with us?" Hedron shook his head. He too longed to hasten after Galen, to stop the tall, beautiful figure as it walked away in the fading darkness.

"You cannot follow him, my brother, for only he can decide to stay. Yet, if he goes on this journey, he takes all our people with him." In two hours' time the building would be filled with the hosts of worshippers and afterwards there would be a gathering of all the Counsellors. They would talk of Galen's journey and his choice to go alone. How could they, in all the lightness of their united being, restrict the grace to choose? Yet how unthinkable to pursue the knowledge that might open up the power to encounter division. "We can only follow him with our hearts." Hedron paused. "And wait."

Galen felt the thread of their love as he sped by the silent dwellings and headed towards the woods across the meadows. How different the walk seemed now from that earlier expedition with Nathan and Rachel. He was glad of his warm cloak for the morning air was cool and the breeze damp and chilling. Although he knew he was alone he could not help glancing around from time to time, checking the empty shadows and vacant grasses. He did not know why he felt a sense of another presence, why he should think that someone followed him when he knew that no-one else would break these resting hours except the Counsellors he had left behind. For a moment he wished he had heeded the advice of Anna and not journeyed alone.

"Why," he said aloud, "I have done this walk so many times, I know each step and need no companion to lighten the journey." He had not realised the depths of his loneliness until he spoke and his voice spun into the twilight like a lost echo. Was that a slight rustling of trodden leaves? He turned round and gazed behind. Nothing. "The light rises above me," he thought, "and I search only for the boy with lost eyes who called to me from the other side of the wall so that I could pull him up. Then I was young and could not help him, but now I have the strength."

Dawn seemed slow in breaking through that morning and the way to the valley appeared rougher underfoot. When at last he reached it, the trees looked fragile in the gloom. Some scattered twigs lay on the ground, mute in separation. Galen knelt to touch a piece of the fallen bark, attracted to a shape that reminded him of a carving he had made in the workshops at school when he was a boy. A flood of memory swept over him but, even as he held his hand towards the piece of wood, something brushed softly against his face and he jumped to his feet, rubbing his cheek vigorously.

"What was that, is there someone here?" There was no answer. He closed his eyes and saw before him the Centre of Worship filled with his people. They were holding out their arms. Stretching his own arms wide, he lifted his face to the emerging sun, so that his curls tumbled to his shoulders, and his eyes shone with emotion. "I am coming," he cried, "I shall soon be back amongst you." The sun surged into the sky, dispelling the darkness from the valley with instant power. Galen lowered his arms and gazed down towards where the sloping land led to the plain. "But first I must finish my journey."

The Tree burst into life as he descended. It floated upon the last remnants of morning mist, rising up out of the vapour in an abundance of spreading branches and glistening leaves. Galen's eyes gleamed with joy as his pace quickened. The scent of the icy River filled the air and its song seemed to reflect his own excitement.

The plain looked vaster than ever, but it was dwarfed by the height of the Tree. Galen started to walk faster, but suddenly the ground beneath his feet started to tremble, whilst in the distance a roaring sound came from the mountains. Even as he hesitated he thought he saw clouds of snow, although he was too far away to be certain. As he stood transfixed he gazed intently at the Tree; surely the shifting earth would topple some of the fruit, would shake an apple from its leafy protection? Although he was still some distance from the trunk, into his mind came a clear picture of the motionless branches, the fruit succulent upon them, skins perfect in their gleaming roundness. He ran his tongue over his lips, across his teeth.

The plain was still again and the Tree had not stirred. He pressed forward, never taking his eyes from its magnificence, gasping with renewed wonder as it appeared to spread ever wider, ever higher, the fruit glinting with moisture in the early light. At last he reached the circumference of its shade and fell upon his knees in gratitude.

The plain was hushed now. Even the sound of the River seemed silent and the mountains were mute again, locked in their frozen world. Galen closed his eyes and began to chant the words of the Celebration of Awakening, longing to raise the notes as high as the branches, to pour out his praise with such resonance that it would reach the ears of his people and mingle with their song. Breathing deeply he tried to magnify his voice, but the sound was overwhelmed by the surrounding emptiness and it fell away into the air like a wingless bird.

He faltered, opening his eyes slowly even as his tongue

sunk flatly in his mouth. He looked across the way he had come and rubbed his eyes to clear his vision.

Something was heading towards him over the plain. He rose, never taking his gaze from the moving object. He stood as if bewitched, hair tumbling towards his shoulders, the darkness of the great trunk behind him emphasising the whiteness of his garments. Over the damp grasses it glided, slim, upright, moving forward almost without motion, fixed on its purpose to reach the Tree and Galen. As it came closer he could see its eyes staring unfalteringly at him, willing him to lose himself in their beseeching depth.

It was Anna.

The sun was growing stronger now and soon the blanket of vapour would be burnt away and the whole plain etched in burgeoning light. Galen and Anna ran into to each other's arms, forgetting in their joy to exchange the traditional signs of love, instead kissing each other with random hunger, lips meeting lips in urgent need.

"Anna, Anna, my love, you should not have come." He ran his hands through her hair, gazing at her face with rapture.

"I had to follow you, Galen, to ask you once more not to travel alone."

"You know I must go alone; oh, you should not have come, Anna." Yet even as he spoke, tears of joy that she was with him started to his eyes.

"Galen, come back and talk with the Counsellors. If it is right for you to search for the wall and the long-ago boy, they will know."

"No!" Galen's eyes shrank into his head with the vehemence of his reply and Anna started back. "No," he repeated more gently, "I have begun my journey and, until I have completed it, I cannot retrace my steps. I go in the way of the light."

"The way of the light leads outwards, away from individual

vision to shared sight. Come back with me to our people."

This time he did not answer. He stood staring towards the mountains. The beauty of his face matched the morning splendour: the blue eyes, the fine ivory features, the blond-white curls framing his face. The pink tongue crept from his mouth and moistened his lips and his hand, which she tried to take in hers, was curled in knotted veins. She knew she had failed, that perhaps she had been wrong to come. His initial delight at seeing her seemed to have changed to an even more fixed determination to travel on alone. Why had she not gone to one of the Counsellors last night instead of lying awake hour after hour?

Galen turned to her and, for a moment, she felt a flood of relief, for he was smiling and the tension had gone from his body, leaving his form as graceful and fluid as ever. He held out his hands to her.

"Let us worship together before you return, then you may go to them and say I will follow soon after, never to leave them again."

As Anna held out her willing hands to her husband, a small rustling sound above their head made them both pause.

"The fruit," breathed Galen, "it is moving."

The apple dropped to the ground by their feet, sunset red, and lay unblemished on the ground. Galen held his arm to his eyes whilst his lips moved wordlessly, but Anna stepped towards the fruit, her eyes focussed upon its perfect skin.

Galen's voice was hoarse: "Do not touch it!"

Anna hesitated a moment and turned her lovely face to him.

"To touch it will do no harm, my husband, as long as we do not taste it. I believe this is a blessing; it has been sent to us as a sign that, as you go on your journey, you must remember the way of the light. Take it in your pack, Galen, and, whenever you rest, look at it that it may serve as a reminder of all that you hold treasured in your heart."

The moments turned with the globe but, beneath the Tree, the world appeared locked in stillness. At last Galen spoke.

"You are right, Anna. We must never taste the fruit, but to touch and gaze at it with reverence can only be a blessing."

A sudden tremor in the branches startled them after the stillness of the previous moments. They looked upwards, waiting expectantly, but the fruit hung securely to the branches and no more apples fell to their feet. Anna dropped to her knees and delicately brushed the rosy skin. Within seconds the fruit lay upon her outstretched palm, deep red against the whiteness of her flesh.

"Take it and carry it safely with you."

As if in a trance, Galen allowed her to place the apple on to his own flattened hand. He stared at it for a few moments, then slowly his fingers lifted to bow over his palms, closing tightly round the fruit. Smooth and cool to the touch, it glinted between the bars of his fingers as the sun rose ever more steeply into the sky.

Anna was leaving. Galen had wrapped the apple in a cloth he carried in his pack and had placed it carefully at the bottom of his sack. Neither wished to say goodbye but both knew that the farewell must be taken. Now they exchanged the customary signs of love before putting their arms around one another and pressing their damp cheeks close together.

"Bless you, Galen, and bring you swiftly back to all of us, your journey safely accomplished."

"Go now, dearest Anna, with my love and greetings to our people. I will watch you cross the plain and then I will leave. Do not doubt me; I will soon return."

There was no more to be said. She walked slowly from him, head bowed as she left the shelter of the Tree. After she had gone a little way she paused and turned to look at him again. He stood before the vast trunk his arms held wide in farewell. For a moment a trick of the light made it appear as if he were pinned against the wood, but then he moved his arm to wave again and she saw that he merely leant against the body of the bark as if deeply tired.

Walking back towards home, Anna lifted her head as she prayed aloud, forming the ancient words and those of her own in a spontaneous outpouring. Yet, even as the sounds left her mouth, an underlying sensation in her mind distracted her from concentrating fully. She reached the edge of the plain but she did not turn again to look once more at the speck of her husband, for she could not bear to see him shrunk so far from her sight. She began the ascent of the valley, glancing from time to time at the trees swaying on either side of her.

What thought had stolen into her mind? As she struggled to avoid it, the memory burst upon her: it was Galen's hands. She had not noticed any sign of his injuries for years but, as she stepped back from their parting embrace she saw that the old wounds, long ago faded, were shockingly changed, so that the livid red and purple of the scars now marred the flesh making it ugly.

## Chapter 8

Galen felt as if he had been walking for hours, but still the amount of ground covered looked pitiful. The plain had never felt so vast and empty, nor the mountains so far away. The River flowed beside him as he travelled, its singing mocking his dragging steps. The Tree's presence seemed to envelop him; he imagined that the branches leant forward as he moved and wrapped their arms around his chest, so that each step he took required huge effort as if he was struggling to escape its wooden clasp. Yet the sun now shone in a cloudless sky and the air wafted the scent of flowers to his nostrils.

He had wanted to call out to Anna, to draw her back, for he realised with consternation that they had forgotten to worship together. Surely she would suddenly remember. He had watched her shrinking figure until he could no longer be sure if he saw her. Perhaps she would turn and he would run to her, perhaps after all he would follow her unbidden and forget his solitary journey.

"Anna, Anna!" The longing words had forced themselves out of his dry mouth but their sound hurt his head and he clasped his hands against his ears. He had not stirred although his heart beat with the desire to follow her. What had held him there, small and insignificant against the breast of the Tree? And Anna had not turned, although he waited through uncountable time, lifeless beneath the hanging fruit. At last he moved, pulling on his haversack wearily as he left, for the pack felt heavy and uncomfortable.

Thus he pressed forward through the hours of the morning, a small, white figure making its way across a vast, green landscape. Where the pack touched his back, sweat moistened his garments and, every now and then, he rubbed his hands together, feeling the old scars which seemed to burn in the heat of the sun.

It was well past noon when he reached the far edge of the plain. The mountains rose up before him, the glaciers clinging to their sides, deserted ice ways in the marble sunlight. Galen felt exhausted and he sank to the ground where he lay for a few moments, breathing rapidly. The grass was comforting against his face and gradually his body relaxed until he felt strong enough to ease himself into a sitting position. He removed the pack from his shoulders and wiped the moisture from his eyes until he could gaze back over the route he had come.

The Tree looked far away, alone in its magnificence. Galen strained his eyes; surely before, when he had stood by the foothills of the mountains, the Tree had seemed closer and he had been able to see beyond to the other side where the path led up to the valley and on towards home? He knelt holding out his arms; if he waited he would soon be able to make out the plain beyond the Tree and the path across it, the path that led to his people. But gradually his eager hope gave way to disappointment for, despite the sunshine, the more he gazed the darker the distance became. He must be even more tired than he had thought and it was affecting his vision.

He knelt for a long time whilst he chanted aloud the prayers of Adoration and Asking, of Remembrance and Acceptance. When finally he rose to his feet his weariness had evaporated and his vision cleared. Now at last he could see across to the other side. Tossing back his head with relief, Galen laughed aloud so that his face shone with pleasure.

It was time to continue his journey. He lifted his pack, surprised once more at its weight, wishing to abandon it, knowing that he could not manage without it. Besides, the apple lay there, safely wrapped in the cloth, a reminder of all that he held dear and, with that thought, he pulled the straps over his shoulders, wincing slightly at the load. He wished to move but still his feet remained rooted to the ground. There was something at the fringes of his mind that troubled him, something seen and yet not noticed, something missing and yet apparently in place. He must remember what it was.

The memory nudged closer into his mind: it was the Tree, something about the Tree. In sudden fear he stared once more across the plain to where the trunk sprang from the depths of the earth. Now, despite the distance, he could see every detail silhouetted against the sharp blue sky. More beautiful than ever the Tree stood motionless and yet... he stared until the pain in his eyes was almost intolerable. Then he saw what had stolen unbidden into his mind.

The fruit had disappeared. The branches spread their arms as wide as ever and light shimmered upon them, but the apples that always hung securely in their leafy cradle were there no more.

Anna was nearly home. She had walked blindly, all her thoughts concentrated upon Galen, and the last sight of him, standing unmoving against the Tree. The wounds upon his hands seemed to sear her brain with their imprint so that she found herself rubbing her own flesh every now and then as if she, too, had received some hurt. As she approached the first buildings, she wondered how it had taken her so long to cover the distance between the Tree and home. In her concern for Galen she must have lost her way, must have been wandering around in circles for hours. It was almost time for Evening Worship and Rachel and Nathan would long since have been home from school. Of course they would be cared for, but it was unheard of for a child to return to an empty house. They would wonder where she was and she trembled to think that she had unwittingly done what no member of their people would ever do.

She quickened her pace and soon the Centre of Worship shone before her. The people were flowing towards the building, host upon host of quiet figures, raising their arms high as they walked into the building. Although Anna moved urgently she was the last to enter and she felt conspicuous and uncomfortable. She looked around for Nathan and Rachel and saw them almost immediately, standing by one of the Counsellors. Nathan was looking at her gravely. She wanted to call out to him, to run and take him in her arms, but she dare not break the silence. The people were waiting; they watched her, their eyes deep with love. Slowly she raised her hands, lifting her face to the light as she did so, and a moment later the voices filled the air, soaring in harmony to the invisible heights above.

Yet they knew that one of their people was missing and, in the purity of their concern, they willed him back into their centre, feeling the threads of love that spun out into the night, stretching far beyond the Tree to where he journeyed. Only Nathan and the Counsellors sensed the threads weakening, and only they saw in their minds the Tree, soaring high on the plain, and heard a rustling amongst its branches that was not caused by any breeze.

Galen paused on the path that led through the foothills of the mountains. He remembered his youthful joy when, travelling with his grandmother, he had cried aloud with exhilaration at the ground rising above him and the blue panoply of the sky beyond. Now, although the sky was azure immediately overhead, towards the west he could see banks of grey clouds moving towards him, flecked in places by a brooding black.

It was late afternoon and he had not eaten all day. As he walked he pushed the memory of the Tree out of his mind. He persuaded himself that he had been mistaken, that he had been much too far away to see anything clearly at all, or that a trick of the light had obscured his vision. Only one apple was missing from the abundance of fruit that hung upon the Tree and that lay safely in his pack.

Weariness had returned to his bones, more potent than before, and he knew he must have some refreshment. He looked around for a resting place. The grass was wirier here and, in the far distance, he could hear the faint roar of the water erupting from the foot of the nearest glacier. The hillside was strewn with rocks and he sank upon one of these, leaning his brow upon his hands, feeling in them the throbbing that seemed to beat in time with the monotonous sound of the water. Slowly he removed the heavy pack from his back and took out a piece of bread. Chewing a bit at a time he gazed at the way ahead and tried to discern his route, but he could see no definite path. He did not look back in the direction he had come from.

The gentle touch upon his shoulder made him exclaim aloud with surprise. Gasping, he jumped to his feet and found himself facing a Counsellor, one he did not recognise, a man who seemed as ancient as the rock upon which he had been sitting.

"It is alright, my son; I have come across our land to speak with you. I have been travelling many days but, now I have reached this place, my quest is fulfilled."

The two men held each other's gaze for a long moment, the blue eyes of Galen startling in their brightness, the silver depths of the Counsellor's stare soft in its understanding. At last they inclined their heads and raised them again before embracing, pressing their cheeks together, placing their lips in turn upon the other's forehead. Only after the solemn greeting did Galen speak again.

"Father, I only started my journey this morning; how could you have been walking for so long?"

The old man smiled and touched Galen's hand.

"Perhaps you called me without knowing."

"Ah." The sigh shivered between them.

"Your hands, Galen, how came those marks?"

"How do you know my name when we have never met before?"

"I am a Counsellor; it is my role to be aware of such things. And perhaps you have met me without realising it. The wounds, Galen?"

There was something about the ancient eyes that refused evasion; they found their way into his heart and stirred his lonely yearning.

"Long ago, as a boy, I fell. I lost consciousness for a while but, when I regained awareness, blood was streaming from my hands."

"Is that all you have to say, my son?"

Galen found himself in the arms of the old Counsellor, his wet cheek upon his ancient shoulder. He felt a healing hand pass through his white curls.

"There was a wall from which I tumbled and there was a boy with lost eyes."

Now the Counsellor placed his bony hands upon Galen's shoulders and held him firmly, meeting the younger man's eyes with his own unfaltering stare.

"There is no wall, Galen. Look before you; it would be there, rising out of the rocky ground for both of us to see. Why did you not tell the people this story?"

"For some reason, whenever I wished to do so, my tongue seemed to expand in my mouth and hinder speech. And then time passed and I began to think it had been childish imagination. Recently, though, the image of that wall and the boy from the other side has returned to fill my mind with its pictures."

"And its demands?" The question was staccato.

"And its demands," Galen murmured, stiffening suddenly, stepping back and lowering his eyes so he no longer had to look into the searching eyes of the Counsellor.

"The way of the light leads away from all division and towards harmony." The voice sounded quieter, weaker; Galen did not know that his own eyes had shrunk a little into his head and that the Counsellor trembled at what he saw.

The older man slowly bent his body until he was sitting upon the rock so recently occupied by Galen. Galen stood over him, looking at the wispy white hair, the skull beneath brown, wrinkled, the hands that rested on the bony knees darker still, the black boots dusty from the journey. The older man pondered long upon Galen's face until the younger man cried out in consternation:

"Why do you look at me like that, Father? What do you see?"

"Do you really ask me that question, Galen?"

"Yes, yes, I must know."

"No, Galen, you must not know. Do not forget that knowledge is a gift to be sought carefully, not our right to be greedily demanded. Do you forget our teachings? Nevertheless, I will answer your question. I see a desire for knowledge in your face of things you should not seek to know, for sensations that no person should pursue. I see in your haversack an apple, as yet untouched, wrapped in a cloth."

"But how...?"

The old man took no notice.

"You were born, Galen, with a special beauty and a rare

61

grace. Right across our land the Counsellors have been aware of your fine spirit, the blessing of its potential, and have delighted in the favour of your presence amongst us. But alongside the joy has grown an unease as we have seen develop within you a desire to strip the great Tree of its foliage and discover its sacred secrets."

"No!" Galen held his hands together to ease the throbbing pain. "If you thought such a thing, why was nothing said to me?"

"Perhaps you could not hear, my son, but it is not too late even now. You still have all the qualities that you were blessed with at birth; you may realise the full flower of your grace."

"What should I do, Father? Help me."

The old man stretched out his hand, holding the palm upwards.

"Give me the apple. It is unblemished. I will return it to the Tree. Then your haversack will be light again and you will be able to retrace your steps to your people."

"No!" The shout was uttered before Galen knew he had opened his mouth. "You do not understand; Anna handed me the apple to remind me of all that I hold dear. It will lead me back home; I will never take a bite from it. Never!"

"I understand very well, Galen. You know the fruit should never be touched and already you have taken a dangerous course in bringing it away from its resting place. But I say once again, it is not too late. Give me the apple that I may bear it to its rightful place."

"And the wall and the boy?" Galen's voice was hesitant.

"They only exist if you allow them to do so. Refuse that permission and never again will you walk alone across the plain, challenging the River with your solitary step, gazing at the Tree with eyes that would seek to know more than eyes such as ours can look upon with safety."

Galen dropped to his knees and, with trembling fingers, put his hand inside the haversack. With great tenderness he took out the cloth and opened it, revealing the apple: round, smooth, perfect, not a mark upon its rose and golden skin. Carefully he placed the cloth on the ground with the apple resting upon it. The Counsellor knelt beside Galen but he did not reach out his hand towards the fruit; he knew that it must be given freely.

Galen's hand was moving towards the apple, shaking a little as the fingers curled, ready to take it up. They had almost reached it, indeed he sensed the feel of the cool skin upon his flesh, when something sharp and dry and hard knocked the back of his hand so that he cried aloud and dropped his arm to his side, jumping to his feet in surprise.

"What was that?"

"Galen, Galen, what is the matter?" The Counsellor stood beside him, but the younger man's body was so rigid he could not take him again into his arms to comfort him.

"Something touched my hand, something, I do not know. I felt it once before, in the valley leading to the plain. It is, it is…" He struggled for the words to describe what had happened.

"Give the apple into my keeping, Galen, now, whilst there is time. Nothing is here; see, the grasses are devoid of life and the rocks are bare."

Still Galen hesitated. The two men stood together like carven statues: Galen, tall and fine, beautiful in his white garments, head tilted so that his curls fell to his back, the Counsellor thin, a little stooped now, small beside the upright figure of his companion.

"Do you hear?" whispered Galen.

A faint rustling sound seemed to hang in the air for a moment and then was gone.

"The apple, Galen."

But Galen had closed his eyes and into his head came the vision of Anna smiling at him with such loving concern and sadness as she handed him the fruit.

"I cannot give it to you, it is safe with me, I will never eat of its flesh." He felt the ancient hands clasp each side of his head, drawing it towards the earth. He felt the touch of lips upon his brow and a cheek pressed swiftly to his. "Father," he whispered.

He opened his eyes to seek approval for his words, but no silver-haired man stood there before him; instead, in the distance, he saw a bent back, huddled in its white clothing, heading towards the plain. He opened his mouth to call, to beg him to return, but the plea remained locked in his throat.

He was alone again, the apple at his feet. The azure sky had fled before the approaching clouds and the air grew chill. Galen wrapped the apple in the cloth and replaced it in the haversack. He must find shelter for the coming night; with the early morning light he would continue his journey.

## Chapter 9

Galen had slept little and he was thankful for the first shimmer of dawn. After the old Counsellor's departure he had searched randomly for a resting place, longing for a few hours of oblivion, the chance to forget for a while the journey ahead. Finally, he had discovered a small hollow against a rock and there he slept fitfully, his cloak wrapped tightly round him, his head on the haversack.

He stumbled, shivering, to one of the streams that fell from the jaws of the glacier above. Gasping, he splashed the icy water onto his face, then scooped up some liquid and drank in thirsty gulps. His parched mouth momentarily relieved, he looked around at the deserted mountainside. How different the place seemed from that boyhood sunny midday; then he had felt as buoyant as the leaping spray and cried aloud at the glory of the scene. Now it appeared quite desolate. Even though the dawn filtered through in streaks of pale light, the dusky barrenness around him did not change. Yesterday he had felt sure he would find the path he must take across the mountainside to where he remembered he had seen the wall; today he saw no clear way, for the ground was littered with rocks as if they had been thrown randomly by a giant hand. To walk across that territory, as he had planned, would be a slow, laborious task and he did not have the time. Indeed, he was not certain if he could travel that way at all. The more he strained his eyes to find a route across the stony incline, the more difficult, even impossible, it seemed. He would have to climb up towards the hanging glacier and cross that way, he had no choice. He could not understand how he had gone so wrong.

He returned to where his sack lay against the rock and

crouched down to take out the small loaf that Anna had packed for him. He did not feel hungry but his senses told him that he must eat. He chewed the bread slowly, finding the act of swallowing difficult, and drank some water from the bottle he always carried with him. It tasted stale after the clear liquid from the stream. He did not touch the cloth in which the apple lay, although he pictured the pure skin, unblemished like the skin of Anna.

It was time to be moving. Although it was now much lighter, as yet the sun was muffled by clouds. The chill that had settled into his bones during the night made his whole body tense and, however close he gathered his heavy cloak around him, the cold crept deeper into his being. He must walk quickly; the sun would surely come out later and then he would feel better.

Once more he pulled the haversack onto his back, staggering for a moment until he became used to the weight upon his shoulders. He had gone only a few steps when he stopped aghast. He had forgotten to say the words of the Celebration of Awakening and the horror of the omission was so great that tears started to fill his eyes. He stood amongst the rocks, his white hair falling almost to the cloak clasped around his neck and wept, then he held out his arms and cried the words aloud in a trembling voice, whilst in his mind he saw his people chanting in harmony in the great Centre of Worship.

"Wait for me," he called and thought he heard their answer spinning across the dividing space – "We are waiting" – but he could no longer be sure what was real and what was merely the longing in his heart.

He had worshipped, and now he moved forward with lighter steps. It was growing slightly warmer and although the path ahead was steep, there was now a clear track winding its way through the rocks until it twisted out of sight around a distant corner. Galen climbed steadily, following the route onto more exposed ground. Every now and then he paused for breath, gazing back the way he had come, seeing beneath him the River sparkling and the Tree rising to the sky, its upper branches lost in light. Galen had thought that, as he ascended, he would be able to look down upon the Tree and so see what none of his people had yet seen, its summit, but now he realised he had been mistaken. Although far away, it appeared to rise ever taller so that he almost believed that it still towered over him as when he stood on the plain. The light soared so high that he could not follow its flight, yet the lower branches and the gigantic trunk seemed to throw shadows that spread to the very foot of the mountain up which he toiled.

He began to walk more quickly, a sudden urge to increase the distance between himself and the Tree making him stumble in his haste so that he almost fell several times as he hurried up a narrow path that led to a ridge beyond. He would be thankful for the flatter terrain of the ridge and he hoped that there he would find a sheltered place to rest and have something to eat and drink.

Despite the fact that it had been warmer for a while the sun still lingered behind the clouds and, as Galen gained altitude, so the air grew cooler again. He kept on glancing around uneasily. Although he knew that he was quite alone he could not shed the sensation that someone was following him. He had felt this earlier when he walked down the valley towards the plain, but then his unease had been quite unfounded for it was Anna who came to him beneath the Tree. But Anna was now far away with Rachel and Nathan and their people. For a brief moment he wondered if the stranger Counsellor had returned, but Galen knew that the old man would not come back to him.

No-one else walked on the mountainside. He would resist the temptation to glance behind with uncertainty but would concentrate only on the way ahead.

Despite his resolve, the sense of unease did not lift. He now saw that the path he followed was leading towards a clump of jagged rocks and he realised that he would have to scramble up these in order to reach kinder ground above. The straps of his pack dug into his shoulders and the pulse on his head beat upon his nerves with insistent force. At the base of the rocks he hesitated for a moment before gripping the sharp surfaces, wincing as his sore hands made contact with the stone. Slowly he pulled himself up until at last he threw himself down upon the spikey grass at the top. He had torn his cloak slightly on a jagged edge and his boots were marked where he had scraped his feet over the rough surface, but otherwise he had done no damage. He would rest for a while before he continued towards the glacier.

Far from releasing the sun, early afternoon drove the mist towards the glacier with increasing bursts of energy, and the clear skies which Galen longed to see were still obscured from sight.

He had rested for some time after reaching the beginning of the ridge, eating a little bread and drinking from his bottle, and the long haul up to the glacier had been less strenuous than he had anticipated. Viewed from a distance, the glacier had always fascinated him, but nothing had prepared him for the sight as he stood at its edge. He gazed trembling at the vast wastes of snow and ice, at the rocks that lay scattered on the surface, at the dark crevasses that plunged beneath the crust, at the fissures that ripped across the chill-locked river like open wounds. How could he cross such territory? He had stared over to the glaciers from the plain many times, marvelling at their beauty, imagining them to be as smooth as the paths that led towards the meadows. Now the way looked frightening and treacherous. Yet somehow he must overcome his fear if he was to find the wall. He wrapped his cloak tightly around him as the cold from the glacier chilled his flesh further.

He must cross, yet he still hesitated for he felt that, in stepping upon the ice, he would be leaving Anna and the children in a way he had not envisaged. When the sound came, subtle as a feather's fall, his lips pressed together, preventing a cry escaping from his mouth. It was a rustling, like the whisper of shifting leaves, heard for an eternal second. Then silence.

How fine Galen looked, upright beside the glacier, a figure iced in its stillness, his hair blending with the frosty snow, his eyes bluer than lost summer water. Nothing stirred but the tips of his fingers, clenched painfully against the palms of his hands. It was a long time before he moved. He waited breathlessly to hear the sound again but the deserted silence emptied the air of echoes. At last he turned his head and looked cautiously around.

It took him several moments to realise that the shadow coming towards him was a slowly moving figure. Tall and slim it glided forward, never pausing, never faltering. For a rapturous heartbeat he thought Anna had followed him and he opened his mouth to shout aloud in greeting but, even as the words rose eagerly to his tongue, he hesitated. There was something about the motion of the figure that lacked Anna's feminine grace and, as it came nearer, Galen wondered how he could have mistaken it for the fluid form of his wife, for the person now closing in upon him was a man taller even than Galen, with bright yellow hair and eyes that stared ahead with glittering intensity. He was dressed in the familiar white raiments and his cloak hung loosely from his shoulders. Galen did not recognise him, but it was one of his people; the noise was now explained and he was no longer alone in the wilderness of snow and swirling mist.

In his relief and pleasure he laughed aloud, throwing back his head, curls tumbling down his back, teeth shining, the blood flowing through his veins with renewed warmth.

"Brother," he marvelled as the man finally stood before him, slim and upright, "what brings you to this lonely place as the afternoon begins to fade?"

The man smiled. His lips were thin and pale, his teeth like small pebbles and, when he spoke, his voice was soft, soothing to the ear.

"I felt your need and your loneliness, Brother, and I travelled across the land so that I could aid you."

"But you are not a Counsellor." Galen spoke slowly, not wishing to sound ungrateful, "so how…?"

"Ah, it is not only Counsellors who feel the call for succour from one of our people. It does not matter how I sensed your need for now I am here you are no longer alone. My name is Hiemal. I can lead you safely across the glacier."

"How do you know I wish to cross?" Galen stepped back, astonished.

"Why else should you climb up to this height and this place? Over the ice is the only way to the other side of the mountain. If, however, you have changed your mind we can return together to the plain."

"No." The answer was instant. "I wish to cross the glacier and I would be grateful for your help."

Hiemal smiled again, revealing his pink tongue and small pebble teeth.

"Then it is decided. Of course we cannot attempt it today for it will soon be dark and we need to be able to see clearly to avoid danger."

"But how will we spend the night up here?" Galen pointed to the eddying mist above them and the inhospitable ground at their feet.

"I know a cave." Hiemal spoke quietly and with easy confidence. "It will protect us, especially if we stay close together as we sleep."

Weariness had overwhelmed Galen once more and he asked no further questions but followed his companion obediently away from the glacier, down a path towards a crop of rocks.

"My name is Galen."

"Yes." The reply floated through the air as if the voice had life of its own. "I know. You are Galen, Galen Nodeef."

The cave was dark but it was a relief to be out of the bitter air. As his eyes became accustomed to the gloom, Galen saw that there was a bed of leaves in one corner and that the cavern was high enough for a man to stand upright.

"I have some candles in my haversack," he suggested to his companion.

"No." The reply was emphatic. "We can manage without light. We will soon sleep and meanwhile we can see what we need to see."

Galen dropped his pack upon the floor, sighing with relief as the weight was removed, although his shoulders still ached.

"I have a little food I can share with you, bread and some cake."

Hiemal dropped to a squatting position.

"Good, open your haversack." He sounded eager but, when he held the bread in his fingers, he merely toyed with it, nibbling at the edge half-heartedly. "Have you nothing else to eat, Galen, something a little more refreshing?"

"Nothing."

Somewhere at the far reaches of the cave was the sound of dripping water, insistent in its dull monotone.

"Nothing?" Hiemal stretched out his hand towards the pack as if to explore its depths.

"Do not touch!" The words echoed round the cave, glancing back to Galen's ears in mockery – touch, touch, touch.

"Then there is something else?"

"There is nothing else to eat, but…"

"Ahhh." Hiemal's voice was just breath in the still air.

"I have a piece of fruit, but it is not to be eaten."

"Show me!"

It was a command. As if in a dream, Galen carefully drew the cloth from the bottom of the haversack. Slowly he unwrapped it and placed it upon the ground so that the apple lay on its soft folds, shining in the dusky air.

"Ah." Again Hiemal's voice came lingering out of the shadows. "An apple."

"It is not to be eaten," whispered Galen.

"Of course not."

"I have merely brought it as a reminder of all that I hold dear, a reminder of the teachings and ways of our people."

Galen fell silent, for Hiemal must understand why the apple was so important. He swallowed once or twice and tried not to put his hands together and so soothe the throbbing pain. Hiemal watched him intently, his lips pressed close together except for a brief moment when his tongue tip emerged to lick his lips.

"Of course." The skin of the apple sparkled as if it lay in a leafy patch of sunlight on the Tree. Golden and rose-red, its perfection stilled the stares of the two men until they were carved into the cave's interior. At last Hiemal spoke again, his voice startling Galen out of his reverie. "And yet, would the fruit not give us greater strength, would it not sustain us for the journey ahead?"

"Brother!" The cracked and dry voice of Galen trembled.

"You know where the apple is from and that we may not taste it."

"Who tells us so?" Staccato, the words dropped so swiftly that at first Galen did not understand. "Who says we may not eat of the fruit?"

"Why, it is written, handed down through countless ages, the very basis of our daily lives. To eat from the flesh of the apple is to seek the knowledge that will destroy us."

"Destroy us?" Hiemal never took his eyes from Galen's face. "Then why did you bring the apple from its rightful home?"

"I have told you," cried Galen, "I brought it to remind me, to remind me of what I must do and what I must never do."

For a moment Hiemal said nothing, holding Galen's gaze with unblinking eyes, then he nodded, and Galen felt the tension evaporate.

"Good, good, you have withstood the test well. Put away the apple, my brother, of course we cannot taste it, however temptingly the sight of it moistens our mouths. Put it away and then let us sleep."

Galen wrapped the apple in the cloth, folding the material this way and that so the fruit was fully protected. Then he placed it carefully back in the sack. Hiemal watched and waited. At last Galen turned to him and smiled.

"There, it is safe."

The man took him by the arm and led him to the bed of leaves where he gestured to Galen to lie down. Hiemal lay close beside him and fell straight into a deep sleep, his tall thin body wrapped in his cloak and curled up a little for warmth. Long after his companion slept, Galen lay awake, one hand upon his haversack, trying to see through the shadows of the cave and find some light beyond.

The wind whipped into the faces of the two men as they left

the cave early the next morning. The mist had vanished and the glacier glinted ahead of them beneath a deep blue sky.

"Oh, what splendour!" cried Galen joyfully. Through eyes narrowed against the wind's force, Hiemal surveyed his companion. The white curls blew around Galen's head in a silken spray whilst his eyes glistened with emotion. Behind him his cloak flew like wings and the fine features of his face flamed with beauty. Hiemal put a numb hand to his own skin which was shrivelled with cold.

"Let us move swiftly whilst the weather remains fair."

Laughing, Galen assented, following him with light steps, so enraptured with the sights all around that he hardly focussed on the tall, thin figure swaying ahead of him. At the edge of the glacier they paused. Hiemal drew back his cloak and Galen saw that coiled around his waist was a rope, strong and quite fine, and held against his side by the rope was a stout stick.

"Here," Hiemal began to unwind the cord, "we will rope ourselves together as a precaution; follow my footsteps. We must go very slowly for the ice can be treacherous."

How fearful, how strange and yet how exhilarating it was for Galen to stand upon the frozen river. The surface was brittle but beneath his feet he felt the impenetrable depths, the crushing bulk of it. At the moment it was gripped in a steel vice, but later the sun would soften its surface and its cracking voice would suggest new crevasses, fallen snow bridges, the stealthy movements of something which appeared unmoveable. All this Galen sensed as he cautiously followed in the footsteps of his companion, although he had never been near a glacier before.

Hiemal went cautiously, prodding the way with his stick, checking the safety of the surface. Bit by bit they traversed the ground, Galen marvelling at the subtle mosaic of ice colours as he followed. They were about half way across when a sudden shriek from Hiemal startled Galen out of his absorption with the beauty around him, an appalling scream of terror as the ground beneath the other man gave way and he plummeted out of Galen's sight into the waiting mouth of a hidden crevasse. Instinctively Galen grasped at the rope tied around his waist, groaning with the pain in his hands as it pulled tight, gasping with effort as the full weight hung beneath him. After a moment's intense pressure the rope slackened and, as from far away, came Hiemal's voice.

"I am on a ledge. You must pull me up, but slowly, very slowly. I will tell you when to begin."

Very carefully, Galen lay on his stomach and slid across the ice until he lay peering over the side of the crevasse. With horror he gazed at the plunging depths; it took him a moment or two to see Hiemal clinging onto a ledge some way down, well beyond the reach of Galen's arms. His eyes were raised towards the other man with almost venomous intensity. Galen shuddered at the smell of fear that rose out of the icy tomb.

"Pull, pull!"

Still Galen hesitated. He felt an urge to undo the rope around his waist, drop it into the gaping hole, find his own way back across the glacier, back down to the plain and the Tree, back, back to his people.

"Pull!"

Galen's hands went towards the knot around his waist. The weight of the rucksack seemed to crush him against the ice and his hands burned in anticipation at the thought of the friction they must bear if he was to obey the stranded man.

"Oh, my people," he whispered, and he felt the moisture on his cheeks and an overwhelming sadness he had never experienced before.

"Pull!"

Galen began to pull. How could he think of doing anything else? For Anna he pulled, for Nathan and Rachel, for his family and his people, for the love that had filled his being throughout his life and that had encircled their people throughout time. He thought he would be dragged into the void by the weight of the other man but at last Hiemal lay panting on the ice beside him, his thin body shuddering, his eyes starting with fear.

"You are safe now," said Galen.

Hiemal did not answer, merely wiped the saliva from the edge of his mouth. "Why did you hesitate?"

Galen shook his head.

"I do not know, I am sorry. I was shocked with the suddenness of what happened."

Hiemal said nothing but stared at his rescuer through unblinking eyes. Galen tried to look away. Hiemal put out his hand and rested it on the fair skin of his companion.

"Yes, it must have been shock for you too."

Galen shivered and forced himself to speak.

"Shall we continue our journey now?"

Without the stick they moved more slowly than before and Galen trembled constantly with the fear of what might happen, but at last they reached the far side of the glacier. The wind had dropped and the sun shone more strongly. Across the mountainside stretched a clear path, inviting in its gentle, sloping descent.

"I must leave you here, Galen." Hiemal's face was relaxed now, a small smile playing around the corners of his mouth.

"So soon?" Galen was eager to atone for his earlier aberration.

"I too have a journey to make which I must travel alone. I have shown you the way, as I promised." The long, thin hand stretched out for a brief moment and touched one of Galen's. "You must take care of those old wounds; they could burst open again."

He was gone, heading off in a direction straight across the mountain towards huge rocks in the distance, his form gliding swiftly from view, and he never turned back or paused in his passage. Galen stood watching, struggling to work out what was troubling him, to remember what was missing. Then he knew.

"Brother, Brother, come back!"

But Hiemal did not hear and Galen held his arms wide in concern. They had not exchanged the traditional gestures of parting; indeed, now he thought about it, neither had they greeted each other in the way of their people when they had met. In the unusualness of the situation they had both forgotten.

"Brother!"

No answer came, just the sound of his own voice filling the air with pleading echoes.

It was too late to make atonement and he must continue his journey alone.

# Chapter 10

Galen stood with his back to the glacier and gazed across the mountainside to the distant peaks on his left and then down to the path that wound beneath him, leading to a valley far below. It had grown chilly again and he drew his cloak closer about him, glad of the comforting heat and the familiar texture but, even so, he shivered a little as he stood marvelling at the world before him. From his vantage point he could not tell the breadth of the valley but it seemed to stretch a great distance. If he followed the path downwards away from the glacier he felt sure he would come to the wall.

Hiemal had vanished as if he had never been there. After he left, Galen had stood for a long time on the deserted mountainside. It was still quite early and wispy clouds struggled to make headway against the wind which had returned to snatch at his clothes in sudden gusts. Behind him, the glacier seemed to stir and a heavy mist rose from its surface, obscuring from view the way back to the plain and the Tree. Ahead, in startling contrast, the light of morning was increasingly dazzling and the panorama below him glinted enticingly.

He must begin the descent. He had been so sure that he would find the wall as quickly as he had done that day with his grandmother. The long detour up to the glacier had taken valuable time and now speed was imperative. Yet he remained motionless, listening.

Whilst in company he had forgotten the sound that every now and then startled him with its soft rustling but, now he was alone again, the memory returned. His shoulders stiffened and the straps of his pack dug into his skin. He strained to listen. There was no noise but the wind which moaned in frosty breaths about his neck. If there was a stealthy rustling in that empty place he would not be able to hear it.

At home the people would have already sung the Song of Awakening. Nathan and Rachel must soon be on their way school, Anna to the sanctuary, his comrades to the forest. Sadness tugged at his heart as he stood there alone in a strange place, poised above unknown lands.

In the cave, Galen had awoken to find Hiemal leaning over him, his small eyes staring intensely, his tongue protruding slightly between thin lips.

"Why, Brother, you startled me, is it already day?" Galen had taken a long time to find sleep and, when at last he had drifted off, dreams had haunted his mind. He had awoken shuddering, horrified to see the thin face of another man bending over him in the gloom rather than the lovely features of Anna.

"We must be going, I was about to wake you." Hiemal's voice had been as soft as ever.

"We must worship together before we leave." Galen had assumed the reminder was not necessary, but Hiemal had shaken his head.

"No, no, we are already late. When we have crossed the glacier we will worship together." Surprised, Galen had raised his arms to the roof of the cave, and had opened his mouth to say the words of Jedra. "Hurry, hurry," Hiemal had hissed impatiently, and Galen had obeyed him even as he had known that he should not do so. Later, in his haste to depart, Hiemal had forgotten his promise.

Galen trembled as he realised that, for the first time in his life, he had failed to follow the sacred rhythm of his people. Now he would worship for them both, trusting that his voice would reach the ears of Hiemal, however far he had travelled. Stretching his arms as wide as he could, he cried aloud the words given to the people by Jedra.

As he chanted the ancient prayer his eyes blazed towards the dome of the sky. He held the folds of his cloak outstretched so that they became a part of the air that glanced with sunlight, and his white curls tumbled about his face. How Galen sang that morning and how gloriously the world spun, its peaks and pinnacles, its flowered valleys, its land of richness and abundance, its living water and verdant hills. And so Galen sang, as the sun rose ever more steeply into the sky, until he could no longer hold out his arms and his voice weakened.

He finished, drawing out the last notes, reluctant to cease. A great peace flooded his heart and, for the first time in many hours, the throbbing in his hands was stilled. Although he had determined not to look back, his head turned as if pulled by an unseen thread so that he gazed once more upon the glacier. The mist had cleared and now he could see far beyond. In the distance, arching upwards, were mighty branches.

"The Tree," whispered Galen, "it cannot be, it is down on the other side of the mountain, on the plain." Yet he remembered the previous day, as he toiled upwards, how the Tree had seemed to rise ever higher above him. Then he had thought it a trick of his imagination; now the branches appeared to fill the sky on the far side of the glacier, leaves silver and velvet, the fruit hanging succulent beneath them. He waited awestruck, lost in the beauty of the sight, forgetting for a moment the untrodden world that glinted behind him.

If he left now and retraced his steps he would be across the glacier in a moment, swiftly on down to the plain and across to the foot of the Tree. The apple could be returned to its resting place and he to his, the wall unsought, the knowledge unattained, the lost boy left to his unknown manhood.

Galen sprang eagerly to his feet, his heart beating with joy. He turned for one last look at the panorama he had dreamt of crossing, at the boundless beauty of territories he would never know. The wind had dropped and the whole mountainside seemed at peace.

It was so tranquil, so calm, that at first he did not realise what he saw but, as he strained to understand what lay below, the vision became clear. Far away, cutting across the side of the mountain, was a huge shadow. He strained his eyes to see the valley he had noticed earlier, but it was nowhere to be found. Only the shadow, dark in the sunshine, met his gaze.

It was the wall. It could be nothing else. He ran his tongue over his lips, moistening the dry skin. The choice before him beat in his head and he turned to look at the glacier again, at the way across to the other side and beyond. He could still see the branches of the Tree but the mist was beginning to descend once more. If he was to return the way he had come he would have to move with speed or else he would not be able to find the path. Ahead the sun glowed with increased splendour. Its brilliance dazzled Galen so that, even though he shaded his eyes with his hand, he could no longer see the barrier across the mountain.

He had to go forward or how else could he return with a quiet mind to his people? The wall was there and, beyond it, the man who had climbed up the other side thirty years ago and reached across to him. Still he hesitated. He had so nearly taken the first step of his return journey that the yearning to go home brought tears to his eyes. He stood on the rocky ground wrestling with the agony of the decision he must make. The heat was growing more intense. All white, he stood in a world of sparkling whiteness and bright mist, beautiful in a place of towering peaks and shining ice, fine-featured beneath the inaccessible light of the sky. After a long moment he took a step away from the glacier. He did not, could not, look back. Within a short time the path dropped steeply and Galen began his descent to the wall.

It was the middle of the day and the sun beat fiercely upon the open mountainside. There was no shelter and no sign of any streams gurgling coolly towards the valley. Galen walked as swiftly as he could, every now and then brushing the sweat from his brow, all the time straining his eyes to see if he could catch a glimpse of the wall. He felt very alone and almost wished he had persuaded Hiemal to stay; he dismissed now his inexplicable urge to leave him buried in the frozen depths and thought only of sharing his own uncertainty and discomfort.

The ground was rough and very dry. When surveyed from above it had looked luscious and inviting, but now stones dug into his boots and puffs of dust rose up and made him cough. He was concerned about his water supply; only a little liquid remained in his bottle and he felt increasingly parched. Foolishly, he had drunk unsparingly since leaving the glacier, sure of finding replenishment as he walked, but the dry ground mocked his thirsty eyes and, however much he drank, he craved for more. His lips felt swollen and there was a constriction across his chest; he longed for shade.

He had been concentrating on his own discomfort for so long that it was some time before he became fully aware of something just below him but, when at last he noticed, he gasped aloud, all weariness banished. He began to run, his heart thumping painfully at each step. "The wall, the wall!" he breathed and he no longer felt the pack on his back or the heat of the day. How long he ran he did not know, but at last he stopped and rubbed his eyes, disappointment hitting him with physical force.

He had been mistaken. The dark, green shadow of a dense wood stretched across the mountainside. There was no wall. How could he have been so foolish? Tears filled his eyes and smudged his cheeks. His pack dug deeper than ever into his shoulders and his hands throbbed. He turned to look back up the way he had come but the mist behind him had thickened. He had no choice but to go on. He tried to comfort himself with the thought that the wall must be the other side of the wood and the trees would offer shelter from the sun; perhaps he could even find water there. He started to descend again until, at last, he came to the edge of the thicket.

After the brightness of the exposed mountainside the darkness amongst the trees closed around his face almost blinding him, for no light filtered through the branches. The ground was soft and there was a smell of damp yet, though Galen strained his ears, he could hear no sound of flowing water. Despite this he started to feel a little more optimistic; he was sheltered from the burning sun and, as he was in the wood, he must be making good progress down the mountain. When he emerged on the other side, surely he would see the wall rising up before him?

The trees seemed to grow more thickly as he penetrated deeper. He held his hands in front of him, feeling his way in the darkness, staring ahead for a glimmer of light that would mark the extremity of the wood. Every now and then he rested, leaning his head against a tree. He remembered the forest at home where he worked with his comrades. There, flowers grew in profusion and light poured through the leaves, glancing on quiet clearings and running streams. Here, the wood seemed moulded in static darkness and, if there were flowers, no scent wafted to dispel the turgid air. Here, the silence hung suspended in the gloom so that Galen's breathing seemed an alien invasion, a harsh panting in a voiceless world.

Relief had long since evaporated and now he longed for the light of the sun and the bare mountainside; anything was better than this suffocating blackness.

"Oh, help me find the way out of here!" he cried aloud. He knew he could expect no response, but into the dead air stole a soft rustling close by his frozen form, then something touched his brow and appeared to linger for a moment on his skin.

He ran, or tried to run, bumping into tree trunks, groping blindly, moaning aloud in fear until suddenly the sunlight streamed ahead of him and, miraculously, he was out of the wood and onto the exposed mountainside once more. He flung himself to the ground and lay there for a long time until at last he raised his head cautiously and looked around him.

There was no wall. He appeared to have reached the lower slopes of the mountain where surely the shadow had lain, but no stone barrier towered ahead. Instead was only endless, barren land with no sign of habitation or cultivation as far as the eye could see. He must have lost his way in the wood, must have become muddled in his sense of direction. He felt close to despair. By now his thirst was almost intolerable, but there was still no sign of water and he thought longingly of the cascading torrents that fell from the glaciers and surged into the River on the plain. At least his panic had passed. There were bound to be strange noises amongst the trees; it was his imagination that made them sinister.

He would have to keep going. As he rose to leave, he suddenly realised that he had lost his cloak in the wood. The thought of it lying in that eternal darkness, never to be recovered, filled him with a deep sadness. For the moment he did not need its protection but, when night came again, how would he manage without its warmth?

If he did not find water soon he felt he would be unable to travel much further. He must pause for a few moments and think. The haversack upon his back dug deeper than ever and he slipped it off, groaning with relief as his sore shoulders were released of their burden. He would eat a little bread, it would help sustain him. The thought of the bread brought unbidden tears to his eyes; was it really such a short time since he and the children had collected it from the food gathering? He reached into the haversack and pulled out the remainder of the loaf, yet his dry mouth seemed to discard the offering even as his tongue, swollen with thirst, tried to moisten his sore lips.

He knew of course that it was there. The cloth lay at the bottom of his pack, wrapped in careful folds. Before he was aware of his actions, it lay spread out before him and, resting upon it, glinting in the sunlight, was the apple.

How luscious, how cool and fragrant it looked! Within the unblemished skin the juice must be waiting to burst out and, with each bite, the fruit would quench his desperate thirst. And yet…the teaching of his people, the sacred laws passed from generation to generation, the memory of the Tree, magnificent in its solitude upon the plain, bowing over the fruit throughout time.

"Until I came to the Tree and gazed with longing eyes," whispered Galen. He listened. Would there be a sound as of rustling leaves as he knelt by the apple? The silence merged with the stifling heat and held the world trapped in its white flame. There was no sound, there was no wall, there was nothing, only a thirst that consumed with its terrible desire.

"Eat!" The words echoed around the mountainside so that Galen gazed about in fear.

"Eat!" Now the command was mouthed inside his own beating head.

"I cannot eat the fruit of the Tree," he cried, "it is forbidden."

Behind his clenched eyes the vision grew: beautiful as ever, the face of Anna looked at him with smiling love.

"Eat, my dearest husband, or else you will die of thirst."

"No, no!" Galen's white locks shone in the sunlight, his face carved with tears.

The features of Anna were fading, changing to an image he recognised but had never seen: small eyes that stared and glistened, skin that shimmered but would be dry to the touch.

"Eat!" The words invaded his skull until he thought he would lose consciousness, then Anna stood before him, holding out the apple.

"Is it really you, my wife?"

Her mouth smiled and his heart leapt with love. His fingers had taken the fruit. His lips, chapped and blistered, parted. His teeth gleamed as they closed around the perfect flesh.

Galen gasped as the moisture flowed into his craving body. One bite and he was filled with the sweet liquid, but it did not refresh him. Choking, he threw the apple to the ground, the skin jagged, the flesh torn, its white fruit already turning an ugly brown. The wounds on Galen's hands seeped a little blood, but he did not notice.

Rearing up before him, casting a monstrous shadow, was the wall.

## Chapter 11

Galen's grandmother sat in her customary chair by the open window. There she remained all day, touched by the sweet air that wafted in through the casement and, as evening came, she rested there, still gazing in the direction that Galen had gone. Day and night she stared mutely, never turning her head or closing her eyes to sleep. At times of worship she held out her arms and moved her lips soundlessly, but she never slackened from her vigil.

They came and went throughout the days: sons, daughters, grandchildren, friends, doctors, Counsellors, the old ones. Quietly they placed soft kisses on her brow, pressing their cheeks briefly against hers, touching the old hands that clenched and unclenched on the arms of the chair. She knew they came and was grateful, but her heart had only the strength to acknowledge the loss of Galen and to pray for his safe return.

She would eat nothing, only drinking a little water when it was held to her mouth. For two days and nights she waited and watched. As the third day dawned a slight change came over her. She stirred uneasily in her chair and leant forward, peering ahead intently as if to forge a way through the dividing space.

Anna walked across the lawns of the sanctuary, carrying the mugs of steaming liquid to the mothers lying contentedly beneath the trees. The old ones rested, the new born babies slept and the slumbering peace of the place filled the air with tranquillity. Only Anna's hand shook a little as she handed the drinks to the smiling women. Since returning from her meeting with Galen at the Tree, she had worked tirelessly, at the sanctuary, with her children, pouring out her devotion at the Centre of Worship with urgent praise.

And so she waited, as the precious days of harmony surrounded the people, and the night blessed them with its deep sleep. But Anna slept uneasily, awakening again and again to find her mouth dry and her head filled with disturbing thoughts. Her longing for Galen seemed to invade every pore of her body and, in the dark centre of the night, she listened hungrily for the returning footsteps of her husband.

Nathan threw himself down upon the grass laughing breathlessly. He had been running across the fields with a group of boys and girls and now he shared their merriment as they rested. He pressed his face against the turf whilst his heartbeat steadied and his breathing quietened. It stole upon him unbidden, as physical sensation subdued and his mind became dominant again, the thought that wound around his young heart in tentacles of stone.

"Come along, Nathan," his comrades called, surprised at his stillness, "quickly, it is almost time for us to hear the Counsellor."

"I am coming." He jumped to his feet and ran with them towards the school.

He loved to hear the words of the Counsellors who spoke to the students at the end of the school day, but since the departure of his father his attention sometimes strayed a little, however valiantly he struggled to concentrate. And as he sang the Song of Homecoming, the tears that stung his face reminded him of the waters of the River that swept across the plain, and of his father who had walked away from the Tree towards the mountains on the other side.

Hedron stood at the window of the lofty school hall watching the boys and girls outside. He always enjoyed his time here in the sunny room talking to the children and teachers, and often, when it was his turn to speak, he arrived early so that he could meditate quietly and gather his thoughts.

Today he could not dispel the weight from his heart. Even though the sun shone and the children laughed outside, even though he knew that all across the land the people moved towards the evening chanting that marked the day's ending, he could not rid himself of a heavy sadness. In all his years as a Counsellor he had never before felt this sensation. Could the journey of one man, tall and fine, blessed with a rare soul, cause such feeling? Was he right to see such shadows in the light-filled room?

"Galen," he said softly. The threads of love were still there, crossing the space between them; as yet there was still a bond. "Galen, come back."

The doors of the hall opened. Hedron drew away from the window and turned to greet the children, but today one child entered first and alone, his young face beseeching consolation. It was Nathan.

"It is now the ending of the third day and still my father has not returned."

Hedron placed his hand on the boy's shoulder but, before he could reply, the school community started to arrive and Nathan was quickly enfolded in their midst and lost from sight.

In the forest, the men were carrying wood to the storehouse, laughing and talking in the cool shade, seeing the flowers at their feet and the sky shimmering through the branches of the trees. It was nearing the close of the working day and people gathered together as usual to raise their voices in the farewell chanting. Anton walked amongst them, his bright grey hair contrasting with the lighter locks of some of the younger workers.

"This is the third day of Galen's absence," his neighbour remarked casually, yet there was a repressed question in the words and all the other men turned to Anton with anticipation.

"I have heard that he has gone on a journey and that he is expected back any day." There was silence amongst the group. The birdsong echoed through the trees whilst the leaves hummed of the forest's beauty.

"Why should he journey alone?" One of their number spoke the words but they all awaited the reply with equal concern.

Anton shook his head.

"Wiser heads than I must answer such a question, but I am sure Galen will be back amongst us soon and then he himself can tell us his story."

They listened patiently but still they looked concerned. They all knew that no-one neglected their work unless the reason was unavoidable; Galen had been away when Anna had given birth to Nathan and Rachel, and on the day of the departing of his grandfather, but otherwise his tall figure had never been absent.

"Let us sing especially strongly tonight at Evening Worship so that Galen will feel the force of our love wherever he is."

Anton's words were pleasing to his listeners and they continued through the forest with lighter steps. Anton, however, waited behind for a moment, leaning against the comforting breast of one of the trees.

"Oh, where are you my brother, and when will you return to your people?"

Cloakless in the warm evening breeze, the people moved towards the Centre of Worship. They were a flowing river of brightness in the clear night air, white upon white, host upon host, preparing themselves for encounter, entering the building with arms outstretched as they passed through the great doors. In the centre stood the ancient table and, above all things, shone the light, impenetrable, unfathomable.

The shout of praise rang across the land. On and on they sang the ancient words as, with one accord, they remained there throughout the night, offering their worship until the first glimmer of dawn in the east heralded the approach of the new day.

At the very heart of their outpouring was the awareness of their missing companion and the need to draw him back amongst them with their love. They were many, yet one soul absent left a gap like the space amongst the branches of the Tree when the apple had fallen to the ground. So the night withdrew in wisps of mauve and grey and the people emerged into the morning light. They had never before remained in the Centre of Worship for so long together, but never before had one of their people been missing without explanation. Surely now, when such love flowed out towards him, Galen would return?

Upon the plain, the Tree stood locked in silence, untouched by any wind. Its upper branches soared out of sight, whilst the lower boughs arched over the rose and golden fruit which hung in globes of sunshine. The River flowed swiftly, coursing across the plain in refreshing coolness, and a medley of flowers nestled in the grasses.

The Tree held its fruit with leafy hands, its roots deep in the earth, and so it stood listening to the song of the River whilst it kept vigil, and no branch stirred or leaf rustled throughout all that waiting time.

## Chapter 12

Lukas Galbraith bit deep into the apple. He chewed slowly, savouring the taste of its flesh, rolling the piece of fruit around his mouth, pressing it with his tongue so that the juice trickled down his throat. He gazed gloomily out of the window. It was mid-afternoon, late autumn drear, and drizzle streaked dirt across the panes of glass whilst, in the distance, smoke from factory chimneys hung limply in the sky. From this height the whole town fell away beneath him, its buildings and roads a distant suggestion of other lives over which he seemed suspended in a vacuum of emptiness.

He had been at his desk for hours, trying to reach a point where he could stop thinking for a few minutes. Now, at last, the phones were silent and the door remained closed. He stretched out his long legs and sighed deeply. He felt very tired, and old beyond his forty years. He glanced at his watch; it crept in time with the afternoon, but surely it must reveal evening at last and release him.

He looked at the apple in his hand; it had been so smooth and rounded before he had taken the first bite but now his teeth marks had broken up its symmetry. He bit again and exclaimed aloud in disgust, spitting out the flesh into his hand. He noticed then what he had failed to see before, that part of the fruit was bruised and rotten.

On his desk a cup of cold coffee stood uninvitingly, its surface a muddy grey. He took a gulp before wrapping the pulp of the apple in a tissue and throwing it into the waste paper basket. Grimacing, he ran his tongue over his teeth; despite the coffee he could still feel some of the flesh around his gums.

He knew he must work again and he rubbed his eyes

trying to pull himself together. Pale and passive, paperwork waited in his filing tray; if it possessed a thousand mouths, it could not shriek its demands more loudly, yet Lukas remained motionless. The computer buzzed in front of him. All throughout the vast building, similar work would be going on; the offices were filled with figures moving through their days observed by clock faces. How often had he walked along these corridors of carpets and steel, to glimpse, through half-open doors or sheets of glass, the reflection of his own unwilling toil?

He rose and went to the window. He had a headache and the nagging constriction across his chest was there again. Outside the last light had faded and darkness enveloped the building. Although he had longed for the coming of night so that he could go home, Lukas loathed these evenings when blackness dropped from the sky and swallowed up the meagre daylight.

"I'll hand in my notice," he determined, even as Claire's face came into his mind, disbelieving in her anger at his irresponsibility. Shadow rebellion. He would never find another job that rewarded him financially as this one did. Wearily, he went and stood at the window, running his fingers through his neatly cropped black curls. It was the weekend and he would go home; the work would have to wait until Monday.

The traffic was on the stampede. Lorries loomed out of the darkness as Lukas accelerated, forcing his way into the outside lane whilst, on the other side of the motorway, an onslaught of lights cut through the night at dazzling speed. They pinpointed his eyes and features, though the black curls were lost in the shadowy interior of the car. His hands steered as if automated by a separate will. On and on he sped, mile upon mile of wet, swirling darkness rushing towards him, on and on, racing past unknown towns and villages, unseen tracts of land, unheard hordes of people, on and on as he hunted with the pack for home. Just as he was beginning to think he must have missed his exit, it appeared out of the darkness, and a few moments later he was turning into his own drive. He was home. He took a deep breath and opened the car door.

"Here!" he called to the silence that greeted him as he stepped into the hall. "Please," he thought.

A light shone from the kitchen and she stood there at the stove stirring something in a saucepan, something that smelled vaguely of damp cloth. She was still beautiful, although lines etched the corners of her mouth.

"Oh, hello. I've left you some supper; I've had mine. I'm just about to leave."

"Claire." She looked at him, doubt in her eyes. "Do you have to go?"

"I did tell you last night, Lukas." She tried to smile. "Would you put the children to bed at the usual time? They're watching TV at the moment."

He leant to drop a kiss on her brow as she passed, but something made him hesitate and she walked away from him untouched. After she had gone, he went into the television room where the children sat mute before the screen.

"Hi, Dad." Stephen did not turn as he greeted his father, and Lukas went and ruffled his son's hair. Susie's eyes were glazed, but she held out a sticky hand towards him.

"Hello, where's mum?"

"She's gone out for a while. Nearly time for bed, you two."

Lukas did not wait to hear their cries of protest.

The children were asleep upstairs, but still he felt alone and uneasy. The house seemed cold and empty. He would go and wash, shake himself out of this state of mind. He went up to the landing and fumbled for the bathroom light. It was a relief to stand in front of the mirror and see his own familiar reflection; his white face and black curls showed up the deep green eyes that stared back at him from the glass. His shirt looked a little crumpled and there was a mark on the collar. He stripped quickly, running the cool water into the basin until the overflow gurgled, then he splashed his face and torso, gasping with pleasure. He threw on a fresh shirt and went to find the meal left for him by Claire.

He had eaten and wished that he had not bothered, for the food lay heavily on his stomach. Now he sat upright in a chair, watching the news, shuddering at the images of violence and pain. At last he could tolerate it no longer and turned it off.

"No wonder I have nightmares," he muttered. "Where is Claire? She should be home by now."

"I'm here," she said, standing in the doorway, coat half off, "I thought you'd be in bed."

"I was waiting for you. Where have you been?"

She did not reply.

Lukas flung open the window and gazed at the stars; they had appeared at last, as the temperature dropped and the clouds disappeared. They glinted like the Christmas lights he had loved so much in his childhood. At first he thought the shooting star was a plane and he watched it idly, enjoying the feel of fresh air upon his face but, as it flew across the sky, he saw the tail of streaming silver and felt the rush of power pulling him into other worlds.

"What are you doing at the window, Lukas? Please shut it, I'm frozen."

How alike they sounded, Susie and Claire, eight and

thirty, vulnerable in their skimpy nightdresses. He turned and saw that she was trembling. He took a shuddering breath and stepped towards her.

It was Sunday morning again. They had finished breakfast and the debris from the meal lay on the kitchen table, food congealing on the plates as they sat amidst its stale aroma. The radio gushed a love song and, in the garden, autumn leaves hunched on the grass.

"What do you want to do today?" Even as he asked Lukas felt the hopelessness of the question. Claire glanced at him warily.

"Oh, nothing much, try to catch up a bit."

"How would you like to come with me for once?"

"Oh Lukas."

"Perhaps the children…?"

"You know how the children love to mess around at home on a Sunday."

She looked at him through half-shut eyes. He looked so handsome sitting opposite her with his boyish curls and fine white face. Where did he walk every Sunday, hour upon hour, coming back tired and dejected? What was he thinking as he gazed past her out of the window and at the sky beyond? What was happening to them; where had it gone to, the love she had thought unbreakable?

"Lukas, I…"

The sudden onslaught of shouting cut off her sentence as Stephen and Susie appeared in the doorway.

The peace of the building was balm to his fretting mind. Watery sunlight tapped at the stained glass windows but its rays made no impression on the interior. He was the first to arrive and he stood for a few moments at the entrance, hesitating. He wanted to walk straight to the front and

96

unburden himself, but he felt self-conscious. As he wrestled with the conflict between shyness and desire, a figure came towards him out of the shadows.

"Can I help you?"

"Thank you, I'm fine." The banal words seemed to echo around the building and the elderly man looked at him through troubled eyes.

"If you ever wanted to talk…"

Lukas nodded but he could not speak again. Each week he came and each week he smiled at the priest as he left, but until now he had always managed to avoid speaking to him. The other man turned away, touching him briefly on the shoulder as he went, and Lukas closed his eyes.

The priest was aware of Lukas standing alone, intensity wrapped around him like a cloak. He felt his unhappiness, but feared that for the moment there was nothing he could do for him. The tall, dark man worshipped with a hunger that isolated him and made it clear that he wanted no contact with anyone else. Despite this, when he stood saying goodbye to people as they came out, he kept glancing to the door hoping to see the stranger and have the opportunity of speaking to him again. He waited several minutes after everyone else had left, but no-one appeared. The priest went back inside, thinking that the man must still be there, but the building was empty. He felt unaccountably disturbed. He should have been able to help and now, once again, it was too late.

## Chapter 13

Litter fermented in the gutter and the smell of chips drifted from the café opposite, mixing with the reek of car fumes and damp air that hung about the street. Lukas eyed the scene unenthusiastically. The noises clamoured discordantly and he felt an overpowering desire to escape the shoppers and beggars, street vendors and strollers, cars and motor bikes, the endless upheaval of the street. In the boot of his car was walking gear and a rucksack packed ready with sandwiches and a bottle of water. He needed to be away as quickly as possible so that he could cover a good distance before dark. He would not return home before late afternoon.

It was warm in the car and the sound of the humming engine relaxed him. As he left the town behind, the sky brightened a little, and the outline of distant hills became clearer. His heart lifted as he sped towards the rising ground and a smile hovered around the edges of his mouth. Already the town seemed like a distant memory. He pushed his foot harder upon the accelerator and gazed intensely through the windscreen, scouring the looming hills for a landmark, the landmark that would lead him to the path he been searching for through countless, solitary hours.

He had been walking for some time, along narrow stretches of lane, clambering over styles, passing through dripping woods, crawling under barbed wire into muddy fields. He was wet, cold and tired but he must keep going. He had forgotten the maps but then they were of little use anyway; he had poured over them often until his eyes ached, but none showed what he sought. It would be better to walk by instinct, and trust that eventually he would stumble across the path. He'd tried asking the way, although experience should have told him that it was useless. After parking his car he had walked into a village pub. The landlord looked curiously at the dark-haired stranger, and the few locals seated at the bar ignored him, although there was something about the way he stood, tall and fine featured, and the intensity of his questioning, that made them uneasy.

"Nothing here, mate, except the usual sheep and ruined shepherd huts and rain."

Everyone had laughed, feeling better, cocooned in the sound of their own guffaws. But Lukas had not laughed, just nodded gravely and left without a backward glance, ducking his dark head beneath the low door, trying to block out their voices as he went.

"Didn't even buy a drink."

"Typical."

"Weird if you ask me."


The earlier promise of fine weather had not materialised and the whole world seemed webbed beneath a grey film. He was climbing now, rapidly gaining height, but he could not see far ahead as mist clung to the hillside. No-one else was about on the chilly slopes, and he was alone except for the sheep that grazed indifferently as he passed, or a gliding gull that circled above him in the drab sky. He had not eaten since breakfast and it was now late afternoon, but the thought of the hastily made sandwiches in his rucksack did not tempt him. His mouth felt dry and he kept on swallowing, running his tongue over his lips to moisten them. He should stop and drink but he felt an urgency to keep walking, for the days were not long enough and darkness waited behind the clouds.

The wind was rising a little and gusts around his neck made him shiver. In the afternoon twilight the hillside seemed alien, unending; whichever way he turned the mist blurred boundaries, both shrunk and extended perspectives, so that the place where he walked was both oppressively constricting and frighteningly limitless. He had no idea where he was.

It was at that moment he saw the path, winding into the misty hillside just above him, a clear way, a direction he could follow with some certainty.

"Thank goodness!" In his relief he spoke aloud and he started to scramble up the damp grass, wondering why he had not noticed the obvious markings before. The path was there all the time and he had not seen it, although surely he must have come this route before? He mustn't get too excited, build up hope. He'd done that many times before and the disappointment of being wrong always left him weak and dejected.

At first, the turf sprung under his feet but, after a short time, the way dropped steeply and the ground underfoot became increasingly stony. In his haste and impatience he kept on stumbling and after a while he slackened his pace, catching his breath as he looked around. The mist was clearing at last and, to his pleasure, he saw that the sun hung uncertainly at the edge of the clouds. Excitement rose in his chest as he increased his stride again, pressing forward to a horizon as yet unseen, to a place once glimpsed but long since only visited in his imagination.

The cold wind had brought a little colour to his white cheeks, and his hair, usually so neatly groomed, was ruffled and untidy. He was walking more easily now. Ahead, the sky was growing bluer, and steam was rising from the ground as at last the sun pushed through the clouds. Everything felt lighter: the wind now merely a whisper, the pack upon his back, the boots on his tired feet.

It was then, in an explosion of recognition, that he saw

it: water sparkling in the distance, gleaming in the bowl of the hills, giving back the sky's reflection with shimmering light. It was the water and he had found it at last. He gave a great shout of triumph as the sun blazed over him and the warm breeze upon his flesh urged him forward.

He began to run, leaping over the stones like a child, laughing aloud in his exultation. With every step the water became more beautiful and, as he drew closer, he could hear the wind playing with its surface and could see the mountains rising up far away beyond its shores. The pack jolted upon his back as he ran, and the stones snapped up from the ground at his ankles, but he did not notice. His whole concentration was focused upon the blue expanse in the distance and the exhilaration of finding it at last.

"Yes!" he shouted, and the wind lifted his hair and his eyes glinted like the watery fire ahead of him. On he raced, as the waters leapt before him and the mountains soared out of sight, their peaks lost in swirling white clouds.

He was not sure when he first began to realise, but gradually he became aware that, however fast he ran, the water was receding away from him. Frantically he rubbed his eyes, whilst the vein in his brow beat until he thought his head would burst open.

"Wait!" he screamed, holding out his arms in front of him as if to draw the water closer, to bring it flowing across the land in a river of surging life. "Wait!" he begged, as the water danced away from him, turning to dust even as he stretched out his hands.

He stopped at last, choking for breath, hot tears mixing with risen dust as he dropped his head to his chest in numbing disappointment. How long he stood inert with despair he did not know but, when at last he looked around him, the mist had crept once more across the land and the clouds had sucked the sun into their midst. If the water was there it was lost in the late shadows and impenetrable murkiness of the departing day. He must find his way back to the car before it was too late and he was trapped for the night, lost out here where no-one would find him. He could search no more for now.

Slowly he retraced his steps over the ground he had leapt across so eagerly only a short while before. He had no sense of a beginning or an end; he had been walking for a lifetime, he had been moving for a few seconds. Either way it did not matter. Tall and solitary on the bleak hillside, he walked quite alone. Night had come. The whisper of the moon awoke the owl, and the stars started to slip into the sky, but Lukas saw only the ground beneath his feet and thought of the weary trudge back to his starting place.

## Chapter 14

"My grandson is coming to see me."

"That's nice, dear." The assistant looked at the old woman who sat in a chair gazing out of the window; she must be approaching eighty, but her mind seemed as sharp as ever.

"He comes every Sunday night, no matter what."

The assistant was new and still had not grown used to the smell of the place, or to the sense of loss that pervaded the building: future loss as life ebbed away, past loss as loved ones jettisoned decay with false promises. It was a relief to hear that this old lady, at least, was remembered.

"That's nice, dear," she muttered again.

"Yes, he was born good, that one, not like my other grandchildren – they never come to see me." The white hair was still remarkably thick, although the hands upon the sides of the chair were veined and mottled.

"What about your children?" She was ready to go, but the blue eyes held her momentarily with their fierce stare.

"Children?"

"You're not as fragile as you look," thought the carer, whilst aloud she cried brightly, "Well dear, I'll leave you to get ready for your visitor."

The old woman was gazing out of the window again and took no notice; she did not hear the door shut softly, nor did she mind that she was alone once more. Inside her head the script rolled backwards until she was much younger, full of strength and optimism. She had been so excited when he was born. The first time she saw him a great surge of love had swept over her, and she feared for him having to grow up in the chaotic family of her son and daughter-in-law. She hadn't been able to protect him as he went through his boyhood, although she'd often tried to do so. His parents had not known what lived amongst them.

"You'll spoil that boy, Mother," was the frequent refrain from her son, but he had been wrong. The boy's nature filtered out anything false and he recognised his grandmother's love for what it was.

"He had a strong will, mind you." The old lady spoke aloud in a sudden burst of energy. That had not always been so good, his will, for it led him with such a power; like the day when he had wandered off without telling her and frightened her almost to death. Now he was a man the will was still there and, as he grew older, its force scared her at times.

A shadow fell across the carpet; she had not heard the opening of the door, nor his quiet footsteps.

"Hello, Grandmother."

He had come; she knew he would.


Lukas had always loved to be with his grandmother. He had wanted her to live with them but Claire would not hear of it. If he could see more of her he would feel happier, but there were so many demands on his time. She never grumbled, never made him feel he should come more frequently. They had been talking for at least an hour, but they both knew that, as yet, the unspoken words filled the air more loudly than those uttered.

"What is it?" she murmured as he stared out of the window at the darkness of the November night, rubbing his hands together as if they bothered him. "Are those old cuts on your hands hurting?"

"A bit, I don't know why, it's nothing," but she was not soothed by his answer. The guilt was always there at the back of her mind. She waited silently now, for she knew something was going to be said that she had waited to hear for many years.

"You've often asked me where I go walking, Sunday after Sunday, as I've been doing this past year. I've told you no lies, but…" He paused.

She knew, of course, but had never pressed her questions, for he could only tell her when he was ready and, although a part of her was afraid, now the moment had come, she was relieved that at last she would know the truth.

"You are searching for that picnic site, aren't you, Lukas, the one we went to thirty years ago on that summer day when you were just a boy of ten? But you haven't discovered it yet."

"I'm looking for more than merely the site; you know that, Grandmother."

"No!" In her agitation she rose to her feet. "Don't look any further, Lukas; it was the knock on your head that made you feverish, there's nothing else to be found."

He met her stare with his own green gaze.

"Tell me about that day, tell me everything and then I will tell you my story."

"Why have you decided to speak of this now?"

He took her hand and helped her sit down again.

"Because the time has come for my search to be successful."

"You can't will success, Lukas." She was troubled, for his eyes shone with an intensity that made his face seem whiter than ever. "You'll make yourself ill."

"I must find it, or else I'll never be able to rest again."

She ran her hands through his black curls as she had done so often when he was a child.

"I will tell you about that day, and then perhaps you'll know what to do."

The room was all in shadow. The carer had lit the single lamp but its light only emphasised the surrounding darkness, whilst outside the blackness cut off the world beyond. Yet, as the old lady spoke, the scent of summer days and sunshine wafted into the place, and Lukas saw the mask of age fall away from her face like a shed skin, revealing the laughing mouth, the firm features, of thirty years ago.

*You were such an unusual boy; although you played with other children, you always seemed distanced from them, apart somehow, as if you didn't really want to be there. You would much rather be on your own or come round and chatter to me. As soon as your mother would allow, you'd arrive on your own. Hours you'd stay, talking, or listening to stories I told you. I asked you once if you were lonely but you looked at me out of those fierce eyes of yours and I never asked again. It was a foolish question, for we know that loneliness is a state of mind, especially when we're young. I think you came partly to escape from the house, all those brothers and sisters, the noise and quarrelling. Your mother had you so young, she never really coped. That's why I've wondered, as you've grown up, how you've managed with the chaos and mess, the trivia that makes up so much of adult life."*

Lukas stirred, smiling slightly, although he said nothing.

*It was your tenth birthday and I had promised to take you out for the whole day into the country, for a real ramble and a picnic lunch. You didn't want anyone else to come, although I suggested you brought a friend along for company.*

*'Why no, Grandmother,' you laughed, tossing back those black curls of yours with amusement at my stupidity – your hair was quite long in those days and fell about your face – 'why should I want anyone else to come?' That was what you were like, unusual.*

106

*It was high summer and the town sweated in the heat. We were so glad to escape. We caught a bus way out into the country, dropping us off at a place I hadn't visited before, but we didn't mind because it was part of the adventure. We stood at the bus stop in town, our rucksacks packed with the picnic I'd prepared, and I was just wondering which bus to catch when an old green one rattled round the corner.*

*'Are you going...?' I started to ask, but the driver just nodded and we decided to jump on and take our luck. You were so keen to get aboard that you hardly waited for me.*

*'Come on Grandmother, let's go on this bus, it'll be fun.'*

*We seemed to be the only passengers. I can't remember whether or not I paid, but after some time you cried out suddenly, 'Let's get off here!' and, before I knew what was happening, we were standing in a leafy lane and the bus was driving away. I had meant to ask the man about catching a bus back again, but it was too late. I hadn't recognised a familiar landmark for a long time, and now we had alighted I had no idea at all where we were, but it didn't matter. It was such a glorious day that the whole world seemed full of possibility.*

*How we walked that day, on and on, and with each step the countryside became more beautiful. At first we were walking along the lane under a tunnel of trees, but soon we left the road and began to climb across the side of a hill; in a short time nothing man-made was to be seen, not a fence, not a wall or sheep fold, nothing. You kept on running ahead then returning, until your cheeks were brighter than I'd ever seen them. On one such occasion you paused.*

*'Do you smell it, Grandmother?'*

*'What, Lukas, do I smell what?'*

*'Water.'*

*'How can you smell the streams, Lukas? You're imagining things.'*

*'No, no.' You were almost impatient. 'It's not a stream, it's a lake or something. I can smell it in the air.'*

*'You're dreaming, there's no such expanse of water anywhere around this area, not for hundreds of miles. Why, the nearest would be the sea and that's a good half day's journey from our town.'*

*You took my hand to urge me forward and, as we came round the next bend, we saw it, shimmering in the bowl of the hills, a huge lake, its surface empty except for the reflection of the sky and the ripples that etched its skin. We stopped in wonder, our hands still tightly joined, and neither of us moved for a long time. I don't know when we began to head towards the water, but the next thing I remember is walking across a valley of flowers, a great valley that hummed with sunshine and unrolled its carpet before our feet in a medley of colours. I wanted to sing aloud it was so beautiful, and I saw your mouth moving as if you felt the same way. With every step the lake spread wider before us and, as we drew closer, all sense of our route deserted me. Had we climbed or descended? How had we reached the valley without noticing the way we travelled?*

*By the time we stood on the shore we could only look and marvel.*

*'Wherever are we, Lukas?'*

*You gave no answer at first, only stared ahead as if you were searching for something. When you did speak, your words were strange and mysterious.*

*'I don't know, Grandmother, but this place has lain here waiting until I was ready to see it at last.'*

*I didn't understand what you said; you were only a child, but your words were those of an old man. I felt the younger, at a loss in a situation I couldn't comprehend, and so I fell back on the age-old remedy and suggested that we found somewhere to eat our picnic. You smiled kindly as we laid*

108

*out the food and settled ourselves on the grass.*

*I was hungry, but you seemed distracted and ate little. You sat staring across the water and I saw that your shoulders were hunched and your eyes shone with that fierce intensity of yours. Neither of us spoke as we rested there, and I felt sleep coming over me even as I took the last mouthfuls of food. Did I tell you to stay close by me as I lost consciousness? I meant to, but tiredness made me lie down on the ground in a drugged slumber. When I woke up you were gone and I was alone.*

*I started to call your name, running in all directions, frantic with worry, for you couldn't swim and your shoes and shirt lay on the grass nearby where you had been sitting. I scanned the water but nothing floated on its surface and I had no way of knowing what lay beneath. I ran desperately up and down the lakeside looking for you, calling your name. After a while, the pounding in my lungs forced me to pause, and it was then that I noticed a small path leading around the side of the lake, branching, after a while, away to the right across the bottom of the hill. I followed it, more out of despair than any rational instinct. I kept on calling your name until my voice was hoarse. Tears fell down my cheeks and I found myself praying aloud.*

*I saw you then as I stumbled along, lying on the ground ahead of me, quite still amongst the rocks and spiky grasses. You were unconscious and, as I knelt beside you, I could see that your hands were badly torn, and blood was pouring from them onto the ground. As I gazed in horror you opened your eyes.*

*'I'm here, I'm here, you're safe,' I murmured again and again, even whilst I looked around for the help that would not come. 'What happened?' I held my handkerchief against the blood and watched the white linen turn crimson beneath my hands and mark my own skin. You were still only partly*

*conscious but you began to mutter and I put my ear to your mouth so I could catch the words.*

*'A huge wall, taller than anything, throwing shadows over the ground. Sounds like, like...climbed, hard, hard, hurt my hands...the boy, waving, blond-white hair, must get back...'*

*You struggled to get up but were too faint to do so.*

*'Hush, hush, there is no wall. You have knocked yourself unconscious somehow and hurt your hands. Don't speak any more. Rest a while and then I'll get you back to the road; you must lean on me and we'll go slowly.'*

*You closed your eyes again and I think you fainted. I thought about trying to carry you, but knew I didn't have the strength, and I couldn't possibly leave you there whilst I went for help. I waited until you regained consciousness, and then washed your wounds with water from the lake and bound them carefully with a part of the cloth I had brought along for the picnic.*

*I don't know how we did it. I remember nothing of that walk except the terrible urgency I felt, the need to get you back to civilisation and help. We staggered across the valley of flowers, stopping often to rest, on and on until suddenly, when I thought we were lost in a world of complete emptiness, there was the lane ahead of us with the bus trundling around the corner. I was so relieved to see it I didn't ask the driver how he came to be there at that moment, nor do I remember if it was the same driver, or how we arrived at the hospital.*

*The doctor gazed at your hands for a long time, then at me.*

*'I don't like the look of these injuries - they go very deep and the flesh is badly torn. How did the child do this?'*

*It was impossible to begin to explain for he would think I was mad. I murmured something about boyish pranks, and he was too intent on caring for you to ask any further. He dressed the wounds, but you had to keep on going back to the hospital, for they opened again and again as if they had a life of their own, and the flesh parted just when we thought they were healed. At last they improved, and gradually the livid scars faded as, through the years, the memory of that day receded too. I tried to speak to you about what had happened, but you became distressed if I mentioned it and so I decided that the best thing was to help you to forget. As the months passed I began to think that you had, and so I thought until you began your solitary outings last year, returning with a look in your eyes that reminded me of what I'd seen on that summer's day thirty years ago.*

*Now I'm afraid. I don't know what you are looking for, but I'm afraid. I beg you to abandon this search, forget the past, and forgive me for taking you out that day. I'd meant to give you a really special birthday treat, and instead I brought you back hurt and confused.*

The old lady had finished speaking and age had crept back into her body so that her skin sagged once more around her salty eyes. Lukas knew that he could not insult her dignity by deceiving her. He had listened to the beginning of her story with quiet patience for he knew it well but, when she came to the later part, he stirred restlessly.

"I can't stop looking, Grandmother. I'm scared too, but my fear is of what will happen if I don't carry on. Please don't feel guilty; it wasn't your fault what happened that day."

"But I fell asleep!" The cry was anguished, the cry that echoes throughout time, the cry of the consequences of the unchangeable act.

"You couldn't help that sleep. I was led away from you by forces even stronger than your love." Silence hung amongst the shadows and only a slight glow from the lamp flickered in the gloom. Lukas walked to the window and looked out. "I wish the stars would show themselves; I hate this darkness when you can't see a thing."

She was waiting for his story. She did not want to hear it, subconsciously had shunned it for thirty years, but now she must listen, for to sleep again when she should be a guardian would be the final betrayal.

"I fell asleep, and when I woke up you were gone?"

Lukas walked back across the room and came to sit near her. He looked strained and tired.

*Right through my childhood you always had faith in me, and when I grew up you still believed in me, even when you saw the cowardice of my adult compromises. You're right about that day, it was a turning point for me. Until then I had a vague awareness that I was searching for something I knew I wouldn't find in any ordinary place.*

*The day was a dream, wasn't it, from the moment the old bus clattered round the corner from nowhere and took us off, away from the stifling town to a countryside of fresh skies. I sensed the lake, sniffed it on the breeze long before I said anything to you. I knew immediately that something unusual was happening so that, when the lake came into view, the sight of that great expanse of water filled me with awe, but I wasn't surprised, as you thought I was. And I saw what you didn't, the path that led around the lake before branching off across the hillside and, in the far distance, great mountains that towered towards the sky.*

*I couldn't eat the lunch you'd made, although I tried to swallow a few mouthfuls. You slipped into sleep like a child and you didn't have time to warn me to stay close by. I was relieved because I'd never disobeyed you. I looked at you lying on the ground and knew that I must leave you. It was very warm that afternoon, and on impulse I took off my shirt*

112

*and shoes.*

*I thought I would only be gone a few minutes. I had a great urge to follow the path a little way towards the mountains, but I knew how frightened you'd be if you woke up and found me gone.*

*I was so excited as I ran along the path by the lake. It soon branched away from the lakeside and I was running around the lower slope of the hills towards the mountains. I don't understand what happened next, for I had been looking ahead as I ran and hadn't noticed anything. Perhaps I'd been staring up at the mountains for longer than I thought, but suddenly the sun seemed to disappear and a great shadow fell across the ground. I stopped running, bewildered by the sudden change in light, staring at the blackened ground at my feet, afraid to raise my eyes. I saw now that the soft grasses had given way to spiky, coarse growth and rocks were strewn untidily around me. Slowly I looked up.*

*The wall reared out of the ground, a gigantic monster of rock and stone, impenetrable in its massive stature, blocking out the light with its huge grey body, impassive in its reductive force, its destructive denial. I could no longer see the mountains and I beat my hands upon the stones in rage.*

*'Let me through, let me through!'*

*In my frustration and despair I lay on the ground and it was then I heard the noises, very faintly, from the other side of the wall. With growing anticipation I crawled and laid my ear against the hard surface. What sounds flowed into my head! It was music, but unlike any music I had ever known. There was the murmur of voices, but voices such as I had never heard. They filled me with peace and a deep longing, although I could not hear what they said.*

*Now I saw that the wall wasn't smooth as I had thought at first, so that with care I could try to climb up to the summit, even though it was terrifyingly high. And so I began the ascent, shivering a little out of the sun, a tiny figure against a vast barrier of stone. I knew I was tearing my hands on the sharp stones but I took no notice.*

*I don't know how long I climbed, but I had almost reached the top when suddenly I became aware of a presence above me. I looked up and he was there, gazing down at me.*

His grandmother could contain herself no longer.

"Who? Who, Lukas? Who was staring down at you?"

*A boy with blond-white curls and piercing blue eyes.*

*'Boy! Boy! Who are you, where are we?' he called.*

*Before I could answer, he disappeared from view. I held out my arms, forgetting I must hold on and, as I fell, I thought I heard a great cry from the other side of the wall. When I regained consciousness, you were there.*

"And the wall?"

"The wall was nowhere to be seen."

"So you had imagined it!"

"There is a wall that only I can see, and on the other side of the wall is another land that is filled with sounds of harmony and peace. There are another people who may help us."

"Help us! What do you mean, help us?"

"I'm not sure. All I know is that there was something about that boy I recognised. I felt as though I knew him and I'm sure he felt the same about me."

"What talk is this, Lukas? You fell, you had concussion and imagined all this. There was no wall, no boy, only stony ground where you tripped badly and hurt yourself."

He took no notice. He had risen to his feet and was staring out of the window.

"I must find him."

"But, even if he does exist, he will be a man now."

"I will know him and, when I find him, I'll understand what I'm searching for."

His grandmother was silent for a long time, and he thought she must have fallen asleep, but when she spoke her voice was firm and strong.

"We'll journey together as we did all those years ago and, when we reach the lake, you can leave me. This time I will know you're going and I won't follow."

He kissed her, his green eyes pools of fire.

"It is the only way; I'll get ready."

He did not suggest that she was too old to travel; they both knew that the journey must be made together and that she would find the strength to go with him.

# Chapter 15

Claire struggled in with the shopping, bag after bag filled with things that they probably shouldn't be eating anyway. The queues had been appalling, back past the shelves and half-way down the store, trolleys piled so high that the mountains of items sank slowly, re-appearing untidily on the moving belts. She had tried to pack her stuff quickly, feeling the impatience of the man behind, fumbling to cram the packets into the right bags, to separate raw flesh from cooked meats, the heavy bottles from the sliced bread. The effort of loading the car, returning the trolley, driving home through the traffic, exhausted her. Now she would have to put it away; and all that just to watch it disappear without a word whilst the kids stared at the television or sulkily across the table.

The bags stood in rows on the work surface. She looked at them with dislike and sank onto a chair; in five minutes she would have to go and fetch Stephen and Susie from school. She had been busy all morning and the thought of the children arriving home with their demands and quarrels filled her with dread. Outside, a hint of dusk was already in the air. Soon darkness would obliterate even the drab light which now hung dismally at the window; it made her feel very sad.

"I wish I hadn't gone out the other night," she thought. She remembered Lukas's agonised face as he turned from the window. They were both to blame. She couldn't remember when they had stopped talking properly, listened, tried to understand each other. How had it happened? There must be a way back.

With a sudden jolt she realised that she had been sitting

there much longer than she had intended. The shopping would have to wait. Rushing to the front door she caught a glimpse of her reflection in the mirror as she passed, shocked at its frowning brow, its discontented mouth. Is that what he saw? Outside, she shivered as the cold air hit her face. No-one was about; it seemed as if the whole world had disappeared, swallowed up in the murk and gloom of the autumn afternoon.

Behind the school railings, Susie and Stephen stood waiting, a teacher watching them from the main doors. Susie had obviously been sobbing and Stephen looked cross and dejected. Claire took a deep breath.

"Sorry I'm late, darlings," she called as they came towards her, their faces suddenly alight with relief. "Poor little things," she thought as she bent to hug them, "it isn't their fault."

They were sitting together and she was trying to talk to him, but it wasn't going as she had planned. He seemed distracted and, as she spoke, his eyes wandered past her to the window.

"Lukas, listen to me!" He turned to look at her at last and his expression brought colour to her cheeks even whilst his own seemed to grow paler. As he raised a hand to run it through his hair she noticed that the old scars were sore and bruised. "Why, Lukas," she held out her hand towards him, "your hands look really sore. What have you done?"

"Don't touch!" She drew back in dismay, the anger in his eyes crushing her tentative approach. "It's nothing, I was just careless." He tried to sound gentle. "I'm sorry, I've been working too much perhaps, and I've things on my mind."

"That's what I'm asking you about. Let's talk to each other, I don't understand what we're doing to one another, I'm frightened."

"Of me?" The question was swift, urgent.

"No." But the reply fooled neither of them.

"You're afraid of me."

"I don't understand you anymore. There's a look in your eyes that has nothing to do with me or the children; it makes me feel so alone."

"I've tried to talk to you, Claire; you never wanted to listen so I stopped making the effort."

"I'm sorry."

Lukas didn't reply.

How silent the room was. The television stood blankly in the corner. The children were asleep and no sounds came from beyond the house. He looked at her as if for the first time. Her long, dark hair fell past her shoulders and her delicate features were blotched. He had always loved her eyes; brown, set wide apart. She was small and slim, like a girl. But she was not a girl and her tears could not be kissed away with easy compassion. Into the vacuum between them crept unclean images and, in each other's eyes, they saw reflected their joint shame.

"I can't talk any more now, Claire. When I return we'll find time to speak."

"Return!" She leapt to her feet in surprise. "Return from where? Are you going away on business – you never said anything about it?"

"No, not business, it's personal." The words fell like stones dropped from a great height.

"Personal! What are you talking about? This is the first that I've heard of any such plan. Where are you going?" In her agitation she paced around the room.

"I can't tell you."

"Can't tell me?"

"I'll explain everything when I come back. You have to trust me."

"Trust!" Claire was shouting and Lukas grew paler than ever. "How can I trust you if you won't tell me what's happening? I'm coming with you. Mum will take care of the children."

"That's impossible. I'd never find what I'm searching for if you were there."

"Searching for! What are you talking about?"

"Don't ask me any more questions. I can't give you any answers that'll satisfy you. I'm going."

"You're talking nonsense, rubbish!" Claire stood rigid with rage and fear. "I know what's happening; your grandmother is behind this in some way; she's always had too much influence on you."

Lukas's fingers clenched and unclenched as he stood up and took a step towards her.

"Mum, Dad." Stephen hovered in the doorway, sleep standing at his shoulder even as he faced the waking nightmare.

"Now see...!" they cried and heard the mocking echoes of their outburst in the space between them.

"It's alright, darling." Claire was on her knees before the child, holding him close as she buried her face against his warm body. "Dad and I are just coming to bed."

The boy looked over her head to his father for confirmation. Lukas nodded.

"I thought I heard you shouting."

Lukas smiled, trying to reassure him.

"It must have been the television." The lie trickled sourly on his tongue. Stephen's eyes strayed to the television screen, blank and silent on its metal stand, and Lukas saw his son's face wither.

"Come along," he cried as cheerfully as he could, taking the boy's hand, "you'll soon be asleep again."

Claire followed close behind without speaking, thinking

how empty the house would be without him.

She awoke with a start of terror, crying out aloud even as she tried to open her eyes. He was not with her.

"Lukas!" Then she saw that he was standing once again by the open window gazing out into the night. He was dressed only in his pyjamas, although the cold air rushed into the room and made her shiver. "What are you doing?" The moon was shining outside, lighting the sky and illuminating the silhouette of her husband. She turned on the bedside light, fighting down panic, struggling to keep her voice normal. "Please come back to bed."

The face that turned towards her filled her with a kind of horror. His skin stretched so tightly across his features it looked as though it could tear apart at any moment.

"I'm looking for the mountains." The words were out before he could stop himself.

"Mountains!" Claire's voice was a hoarse scream. "Mountains? There're no mountains anywhere near here; are you mad?"

How glad he was he had never told her his story. She was out of bed now and standing beside him at the open window.

"You'll catch cold."

"Look out there, Lukas, you know the land is flat; there are hills in the distance somewhere, but they're only small hills. There are no mountains."

He was silent. She flung herself on the bed, burying her face in the pillow to stifle her futile tears. He remained by the window and, turning once again to the night sky, saw the shooting star.

"I'm coming," he said, and she sat up and turned towards him, holding out her arms, but he stood with his back to her, staring into the night.

On the other side of the house Stephen too stood by the open window and peered out fearfully. Something had woken him again; at first he thought that his parents were arguing once more and he lay for a few moments listening intently, his heart beating rapidly, but he could hear no sound of raised voices and he sighed with relief. He was about to settle down to sleep when he heard it again. It was coming from outside and it was very faint, barely audible, yet it reached his ears with quiet persistence. Trembling, he had crept to the window and opened it. He listened breathlessly until it came again: a soft rustling, as if someone stole along the grass beneath him. In a sudden panic, he closed the window and ran back to bed, pulling the covers around his ears so that the stealthy whisper of movement could not reach him.

"I've phoned the office," Lukas said to Claire at breakfast, "and told them I have to take a few days' holiday."

"Yes." She did not look at him.

"They weren't pleased, but it was agreed in the end. I would have gone anyway."

She turned to him at last. Her eyes were swollen, although she tried to smile.

"Will you at least leave me an address where I can contact you?"

"Oh, Claire." She did not ask again.

"If you go I may not be here when you come back!" she cried to his retreating form. He turned to look at her, small and lost in the doorway, and hesitated. The grey sky and sombre trees had emptied the world of light, and it was difficult to believe that the sun would ever shine again.

"If I don't go I'll never be able to give you what you need." He started to walk away from her, slowly at first, the pace of his steps increasing as he reached the boundary of the garden. She wanted to run after him but could not move. It was not until later, when her mind could focus on the details of his departure, that she realised he had left on foot, with only a large rucksack on his back.

## Chapter 16

Along the corridors of the old people's home nothing stirred but flecks of dust. In the kitchen, staff were snatching a quick cup of tea in the lull after the early morning rush, but in the rest of the building only the distant sound of a radio suggested life as the majority of the inmates dozed after breakfast.

Lukas slipped in through an unlocked back door and crept unnoticed up the stairs to the room of his grandmother. She was waiting for him, already dressed and wearing her old black coat, her white hair tied neatly in a bun. His heart sank as he saw how frail she looked.

"I shouldn't be taking her," he thought, "it's too dangerous." She saw the expression on his face and understood.

"Don't even think it, Lukas." She stood up and kissed him, handing him a small bag to be put in the rucksack.

He felt a boy again, standing before her. Whatever he said, he knew she would come and he did not really wish to stop her. No-one saw them leave, stealing hand in hand down the long driveway towards the open gates. As soon as they were beyond the grounds the old lady began to chuckle and, turning to look at her, Lukas saw that she looked younger, more upright, and that her eyes sparkled with anticipation.

"We'll go to the same bus stop," she said, "and wait."

"You know, I never thought about using the car; I suppose I was thinking about our picnic all those years ago, and just came along as if I was still a boy."

His grandmother smiled but said no more.

It must be his imagination, but the bus that trundled round the corner seemed familiar and they climbed aboard with relief, grateful to be out of the chill November weather.

"Drop us somewhere out in the country, please," said Lukas to the driver, "so long as it's completely isolated, anywhere will do." The man nodded; he didn't seem to think there was anything strange about Lukas's request, nor did he bother to look at him. Lukas put some coins on the tray and led his grandmother to a seat. They were the only passengers but they weren't surprised, it was such a miserable day. The motion and warmth made them sleepy and, before long, Lukas felt himself drifting into unconsciousness; the old lady was already dozing, and it was not until the bus jolted slightly and started to slow down that they woke up and looked around in bewilderment. Outside they could see blue sky, a leafy lane and could hear the sounds of birds calling and smell the scent of grasses.

They waved to the driver as they alighted and he nodded briefly.

"Is it the same lane?" Lukas gazed around curiously. "It looks like it, although of course one leafy lane is very like another."

"We're on the same journey, Lukas, but I hope that it will have another ending." There was a question in her voice which he could not ignore.

"I'm not sure what to expect," he admitted, "all I know is that if I don't find the wall and the boy, who will be a man now, then no future journey in my life will have any meaning." She made no answer.

After a short while they left the road and began to climb along the side of a hill so that soon nothing man-made was to be seen, not a wall or fence, not a distant pall of smoke. The grasses stirred on the hill and the streams ran down its side, but Lukas and his grandmother were alone under an autumn sky that shone as if it were midsummer.

"Tell me if you grow tired," Lukas said again and again, but she smiled as if he had suggested something foolish and eventually she paused for a moment and turned to him.

"I'm alright, can't you see that? It's as if the years have dropped away and I'm no longer old, at least for the moment."

He did not ask the question again, yet how tiny she seemed out there in the open, a gossamer figure in that world of blues and greens, of flowing landscape and arching skies. He prayed that her strength would not desert her.

They were following the path towards the sun. The way ascended gently, round the side of the hill, flattening out through a long, narrow valley that seemed to be leading towards steeper ground ahead. Lukas looked around for the familiar sheep but there were none to be seen, nor were there any higher up where the path led through rocky outcrops towards the deeper sky above.

"I don't remember this way," he said at last as the floor of the valley narrowed at the beginning of a sharper ascent. Now they had reached it, the path looked steep and he could see that loose stones and small rocks would make the climbing even more arduous. "Let's rest a while and have our lunch." He glanced at his watch. They had been walking a long time with few stops; in his impatience to cover the ground he'd been thoughtless.

There was a small stream near the path, with grass at its edge, and here they sat, whilst Lukas took the bread and cheese out of his rucksack. She broke a little of the bread, took a small piece of cheese. As they ate Lukas looked around carefully. As far as he could see, the hills stretched away on either side, whilst behind them the valley flowed towards some distant woods which he hadn't noticed before. Above them, the sky still shimmered blue, but a cold wind lifted his black curls and made him shiver. He felt a great responsibility for his grandmother and wished he had planned their excursion more carefully, brought more supplies. He dug into his rucksack and pulled out a warm jacket which he wrapped around her shoulders.

"I'm fine," she said, but she huddled deeper into the wool and he noticed with concern how sharply the lines were etched upon her face. The earlier, youthful strength had not lasted. What was he doing here risking the safety of the one person who had always protected him? He knew he would never find the lake without her, but she looked so fragile and vulnerable. "You have no choice, Lukas, don't blame yourself. If I hadn't come I would have died of grief at being left behind." She ran her hand through his curls briefly. "Let's carry on, for even if we move slowly we'll get there."

The stream that ran down beside the path, from which they had drunk a little earlier, became more vociferous as they climbed, and the occasional spray that caught their faces was sharp and cold. Racing over the pebbles, through rocks, it leapt and spluttered, frothed white as it catapulted over sudden drops or sank into dark pools before it eddied and swirled back into its descent to the valley below. Cloud was rolling in ahead, mopping up the blue with relentless efficiency.

"I didn't think that weather could last." Lukas had to shout to make himself heard. "We must find shelter before dusk." But he was pressing on, straining his eyes to see ahead, and she knew that he longed to turn the corner at the head of the stream and discover the lake waiting for them.

"Don't hope too soon, Lukas, I've no sense that we are near it yet." He did not answer and she looked at his white face with concern.

The pain of his disappointment hurt them both. As they followed the curve of the path and climbed up the last small rise to the source of the stream they saw before them not a sparkling inland sea, but a small pool shadowed by weeds that swayed under its surface like ghostly limbs.

"Oh!" Lukas's cry fled around the encircling hills, then fell away into the air.

The day was dying and, with the fading light, a harsher chill crept up from the ground and wrapped itself around their bodies. In his disappointment, he had forgotten the urgent need to find shelter and he chastised himself bitterly, looking across the pool to the gorse on the other side, to the hills that rose in unwelcome raggedness all around them. Just as he was beginning to despair, he saw the cave's entrance, half hidden by rocks, close behind them.

"We're alright, Grandmother! Look, there's shelter. I'll soon collect some wood and have a fire going and then you can rest." He took her arm and led her to the entrance; it was dry, although the chill air struck them both.

"I'll be perfectly comfortable here." The old lady nodded as Lukas helped her into the gloomy interior and saw her seated on a flat rock before going outside again to find some wood to make a fire. It was half an hour before he returned, carrying an assortment of sticks and odd branches that were scattered across the hillside.

He looked at her from time to time as he knelt, building the fire. What was happening to her? At times she appeared almost ancient, at times a woman in her prime. Now the glow around her face made her seem ageless, younger than birth, older than time. He could not understand it; he only knew that, whatever her physical appearance, her spirit was always the same, and he felt ashamed of his own doubts and weakness. He would not let her down again.

The old lady was troubled and could not sleep. She stirred restlessly. Lukas had been silent for some time and his even breathing made her think he might have slipped off. She was glad, for he had sighed and turned over frequently when they had first lain down on the floor of the cave in their sleeping bags, which Lukas had packed as an afterthought, little thinking that they would be needed.

"Perhaps I'm just missing my soft bed," she thought, but she knew this was not the reason for her sleeplessness. Although the ground was hard, she was warm, and Lukas had done his best to make her comfortable. And yet…out of the shadow of her thoughts came something that disturbed her.

"Grandmother, are you awake?" For a moment his voice startled her, but she was glad he had spoken.

"Yes, but I'll soon be asleep."

"What are you thinking about? I know you've something on your mind."

She knew it would be pointless to deny it.

"You'll think me foolish."

"Tell me; you mustn't lie awake worrying."

Her voice came out of the gloom.

"When we were walking today, every now and then I had the sensation that we weren't alone. More than that, I felt we were being stealthily and deliberately followed. I kept on looking around, but I couldn't see anyone and I thought I must be imagining things. For the first part of the day, the sun shone and the whole world was so beautiful; if there was someone else out there roaming the countryside, who was I to question that? Later, when it became colder, I told myself that no-one else would persevere in that unpleasant weather. Yet I still felt uneasy and turned to look behind when I thought you wouldn't notice. There was nothing but the empty landscape stretching away into the distance. I saw you glance around at times and wondered if you heard something too, but you never said anything and I hoped that tiredness was making me imagine things."

"But," – Lukas's voice was a whisper – "you're not sure?"

"Lying here, I thought I heard something move in the cave. It was very slight and I was almost asleep. At first I told myself I must have been dreaming, but I don't think I was. I had sensed something in the cave, the same presence that I felt on the hillside today."

For a moment he said nothing.

"Do you think I'm losing my senses, Lukas?"

He laughed quietly and she felt the warm touch of his hand on her forehead.

"I certainly don't. I just think you're very tired. I've heard nothing. Sleep now."

She seemed to accept his reassurance, for soon her rhythmical breathing told him she slept at last. But he lay awake a long time listening, straining to hear if he could identify the sound of furtive footsteps above the moaning of the wind outside, or catch the sense of a presence that watched and waited through the long, cold hours of darkness.

He sat up and peered around the shadowy interior – nothing. Not until he was too exhausted to watch or listen any more, and only once he had sunk into an uneasy sleep, did the form steal silently into the cave again, hovering for a few seconds to gaze at his white face, before it disappeared into the blackness of the night.


They awoke to the sound of screaming and shouting, the noise of explosions and bursts of gunfire.

"What is it, what's happening?" cried his grandmother, waking in panic from her drugged sleep.

"I don't know. It can't be what it sounds like." Lukas was struggling to stand, pulling on his jumper over his crumpled shirt. "I'll look, hold on a moment."

Outside the cave's entrance the horror of the scene before him rendered him speechless.

"What is it, Lukas, what's the matter, whatever is happening?"

He turned to her with an ashen face, moving his lips, running his tongue across the dry skin until the words came.

"I don't know what's happening, or where we are. It's madness. There's no hillside out there, nothing I recognise, but something terrible is going on. We can't stay here, it's not safe. If we're found we're finished!" He helped her from her sleeping bag and to the opening of the cave. She gazed in disbelief and terror.

In front of them ran countless people. They ran alone or in groups, men and women, young and old, small children clinging to the hand of an adult or older child, babies held against the breasts of frantic parents. They were all on foot, shouting to each other, screaming aloud their fear; only those who lay upon the ground, dust splattered, motionless in death or waiting to die in the choking air, did not flee. The missiles fell out of the sky, appearing from nowhere.

"One of those missiles could come through into the cave at any moment. We must go." With trembling fingers, Lukas packed their few belongings into the rucksack; the sleeping bags would have to be left behind. He was almost delirious with the desire to escape, even though it meant running with the stricken crowd. He turned to his grandmother, standing tiny and shaking at his side. "I'll carry you, you can't possibly keep up the pace. God knows what's happened or where we are."

She held out her arms to him like a child and he swept her up against his chest.

He ducked out of the cave. There was no hillside, no stream, no path winding back down the way they had come, just a pot-holed road and a streaming mass of moving flesh.

The noise was almost unbearable. No-one took any notice of them as they joined the fleeing column, but he saw to his consternation that a woman running next to him had blood seeping from a wound on her head and that the baby she clasped so protectively in her arms was already dead.

"Where's the enemy?" He gritted his teeth against the fear of sudden injury, ducking his head automatically as the ground around him erupted with fire. "Isn't there any transport, something to help us escape?"

"There's no help. Run!" Lukas looked around in despair.

"Lukas, put me down and save yourself," beseeched his grandmother as he gasped with heart-bursting effort, but he merely held her tighter and bent lower over her body.

"Never!" he gasped as the sweat poured over his eyes. He could see no end to the road ahead, or to the crowds of fleeing people. "Where are we going?" he cried, but no-one could answer him on that flight from death, although all around him they were dying as they ignored his question.

At last the constriction in his chest grew so great that he had to stop for a few moments. He fought his way to the side of the road where he carefully lowered his grandmother to the ground.

"We'll move on in a short while," he promised and she smiled at him, although her cheeks were caked with dust and her white hair fell untidily to her shoulders. Slowly his breathing returned to normal and it was then he became aware of a small hand tugging at his trousers. He looked down; the little girl standing by his side, trying to attract his attention, could be no more than six or seven years old, and she was alone.

"Can I come with you?" He saw in her face the deathly answer to the question he did not ask. Lukas hesitated, torn between his need to move as quickly as possible and the poignant hope in the child's eyes.

"I'll walk for a while, Lukas, but we'll have to go more slowly." His grandmother touched the child's head gently.

He did not argue, for they both knew they could not leave the little girl behind. He took the child into his arms as if she were his own, whilst his grandmother clasped her hand around his waist.

Back into the fleeing crowd they fell, stumbling forward together. The noise had intensified: the shouting of the people, the blast of gunfire and explosions. On and on they staggered, almost numb with fear, on and on down the grey, pitted road, not stopping when someone fell beside them, not pausing when the explosions shook the ground under their feet, or when the acrid air made them gasp for breath. Not stopping at all until he felt the child's arms slacken around his neck and saw the crimson hole in her temple. Then at last he faltered and turned his stricken face to his grandmother.

"We must try to leave this road; I think the little girl is dead."

He saw that the old lady was grey with exhaustion and that only her will was keeping her going; it was a miracle that she had not fallen long before now. She nodded her agreement. Just when he thought they would die upon the highway, struck down by an unseen foe, he realised that they had stepped off the erupting surface. It was then he saw that, to the side of the dusty route, lay a great forest, unseen in his frantic terror, a forest where the noise quickly faded and the stillness closed around them like a cloak. Why had he not thought to leave the road before? What was happening to him? He must be going insane. They walked for a few moments and then he sank to the ground, the dead child still in his arms, whilst the old lady knelt by his side. At last, he laid the small body down and looked about for some implement with which he could dig a grave.

"How strange," he said as he searched, "it's such a short while since we left the road, yet I can't hear any sound of violence. If it weren't for the child I would hardly believe it existed."

"These ancient trees quickly cover any noise. We must bury the little girl."

He found a large, flat stone and began to dig the soft and mossy earth beneath one of the great trunks that stood silently around them. He dug for a long time whilst the old lady watched, holding the head of the child in her lap, sometimes kissing the wound on her head or stroking the tangled hair.

They buried her amongst the trees at twilight. Lukas placed her dainty body, as if to sleep, into the waiting earth. They covered her with soil until her face was lost from sight. Lukas rested the stone he had used for digging at the head of the grave and his grandmother gathered some leaves and scattered them over the small mound. Lukas whispered the words of burial, struggling to bring them to his memory, whilst they knelt on the forest floor in the gathering dusk. The old lady wept.

"We don't even know her name."

"We must move, Grandmother," said Lukas at last, "and find shelter for the night."

"Let's walk further into the forest, away from the direction of the road; I'm sure we'll find somewhere."

To his astonishment, now that they had buried the little girl she seemed suddenly stronger. He rose to his feet, tall and slim against the trees, and held out his hand to her, but it was she who spoke.

"I'll lead the way for a while; the forest doesn't look so dense ahead. Let's go in that direction."

He still had his rucksack on his back, containing their few meagre supplies. If necessary, they would have to sleep in the open. He nodded his agreement and followed her without speaking. After a few steps, they paused and turned round to take one last look at the grave of the nameless child. How small it looked beneath the arms of the vast trees and how still the forest seemed as it guarded the ground where she lay.

## Chapter 17

They did not know how long they had been walking through the forest gloom. After leaving the graveside they were silent for some time, the memory of the child's face suppressing their words. Tiredness, shock and thirst added to the numbing sense of loss and they longed to sink to the earth and rest. Their water bottle was empty and, as they walked, Lukas searched anxiously for a source of water.

At first the way ahead had seemed lighter but, as they moved slowly forwards, the density of the trees appeared to spread with them so that the light grew fainter as the forest tightened its grasp around them. Lukas wished to avoid a night in the open if at all possible, for he felt increasingly worried about his grandmother. Her earlier burst of strength had evaporated and he could not understand how she was still standing. She looked exhausted and very old; he did not know how much longer she could go on, and he half carried her, stopping frequently for rest.

The journey seemed interminable. In all that great expanse of woodland there was no hint of any kind of animal life, yet Lukas had felt his grandmother's back go rigid on several occasions, as if she had noticed something and was afraid.

"Lukas," she said at last, her voice tentative and low, "have you heard anything, anything strange or unusual?"

"What kind of thing? The only sound I've heard is our feet on the dead branches and leaves."

She stopped and leant against him. Although she looked tired, almost past endurance, her eyes were alert and concerned.

"I thought I heard a slight rustling behind us, as if someone was following us, someone who doesn't want to be seen."

Lukas glanced around uneasily.

"Was it only yesterday that we were climbing up the hillside with the view of the valley below?" he thought, whilst aloud he said, "Is it the same presence you sensed on the hills, the one you told me about last night in the cave?" He knew her answer before she spoke.

"Yes, it's the same presence and it frightens me."

"I haven't heard anything, and I still think your exhaustion is playing tricks with your mind. Why, there was no-one on those hills but us, and who could possibly be creeping through this lonely forest? Do you think that someone from that crowd is following us, or that perhaps the unseen enemy has tracked us down?"

She tried to smile.

"Ah, perhaps you're right. I've been isolated in that home for too long." But her words carried no conviction. They stood motionless together, trying not to listen, yet straining their ears in the hope that she had been mistaken. They both heard the rustling, clear for a brief moment before it ceased, and all was silent again.

"Who is there?" cried Lukas to the empty echoes of his own voice as he spun around, peering into the forest. Nothing stirred. The trees were standing statues and, at their wooden feet, the ground was mute. He tried to sound light-hearted. "See, you're making me nervous too. Let's move on and not listen out for any imagined noises."

Despite the brave words they both knew the sound that stole into their heads had not been imagined, and they walked with an increased urgency. They talked rapidly in order to create their own noise and, as they stumbled through the undergrowth, neither turned to see if any shadowy and silent form followed them.

Just when they began to think that the forest was never-ending, as if it covered the whole globe in a twilight prison, the density of the trunks thinned and, with each step, the air grew fresher until, all at once, they saw a clearing ahead where the ground rose a little, as if pushed up by an unseen hand.

"Look!" Lukas ran ahead of his grandmother in his relief. "Look at that, is it real?"

"Indeed it is," she rejoiced following slowly behind him, "we've found somewhere to rest at last."

The building unfolded from the top of the ground in graceful contours. Its large windows glinted with unseen light, whilst the roof sloped down over the weathered stone creating, beneath its jutting edges, eaves of running ivy and birdsong. As they drew nearer, the great wooden door in the centre of the building opened and through it stepped an elderly man, tall and silver-haired, dressed in long flowing robes of green. He held out his arms to them.

"Welcome, my friends," he said as they stepped up to him, "my name is Naos. You have found shelter at last."

What a joy it was to be led along the warm, light corridors to their adjoining rooms. The simple bedsteads were adorned with crisp linen, whilst on each dressing table a large bowl of steaming water offered the chance to cleanse themselves.

"When you have refreshed yourselves a little, one of our people will be waiting to take you down to the evening meal, if you have the strength, but if not we will bring you something to eat in your rooms. If you wish to join our worship after eating, you are most welcome as well, but if you prefer to go straight to bed after your trials, we shall understand."

"How?" Lukas began, but Naos was gone, and his grandmother shook her head. Already some of the deep exhaustion had left her face.

"Don't ask questions, Lukas, just accept. Let's go and wash away the stains of the journey."

With what pleasure and gratitude Lukas stripped off his soiled clothes and cleaned himself in the sweet-smelling water. As he dried and dressed in the fresh, white garments laid carefully on the bed, he thought with growing wonder about the place they had found. A quiet knock on the door startled him and, when he opened it, a tall, graceful woman of middle age stood before him, dressed in green robes. She inclined her head to him and smiled.

"I'm Rosemary. I have helped your grandmother to wash and persuaded her to go to bed. She has drunk and eaten a little and is now sleeping. She asked me to give you her love and to say that she knows she will rest peacefully tonight. She wishes you to join us for the evening meal."

Lukas inclined his head in return. "Thank you, I would like that, but first, may I see her?"

She lay between the sheets, her hands folded on her chest, her white hair spread across the pillow. Her skin was smooth and beautiful in the softly lit room. He kissed her forehead but she didn't stir.

"Rest well," he murmured.

Rosemary stood in the doorway observing the young man as he leant over the sleeping woman. In his fresh, light raiments, his dark head bent forward, the white intensity of his profile concentrating upon the slumbering old lady, he looked all grace and love. Then he became aware of her scrutiny and slowly moved his head to gaze at her in return. His slim fingers released those of his grandmother and she noticed with concern bruising on the palms of his hands as if he had recently hurt himself. She opened her mouth to express sympathy, but his intense stare made her hesitate.

Instinctively she took a step backwards.

"Please follow me."

He walked silently behind her, along airy corridors, down a wide flight of stairs, across the stone-flagged floor of the large hall where flames leapt in the vaulted fireplace, down long passages, until they reached the dining room and entered its lofty interior.

It was difficult to judge how many people stood at the tables, not speaking, waiting for them to arrive. Lukas looked at the rows of figures in wonder, at the ceiling of richly carved wood, at the room washed with the scent of flowers, the great tables laid ready for the communal meal. At the far end stood Naos, and it was to his side that Rosemary led Lukas. The gentle smile of the elder man welcomed him and, when he had taken his place, everyone bowed their heads. Then Naos held out his arms and said words of thanksgiving, and Lukas felt his own lips moving in unconscious echo.

There was no speaking during the meal. In ordered rows they filed to collect bowls of steaming soup, plates of rice and vegetables, cheese and bread. Lukas ate slowly, savouring each mouthful of the delicious fare and the silent friendship and companionship of those around him. When the meal was finished and the tables cleared, they all returned to their places and stood behind their chairs once more, joining in the thanksgiving led by Naos's quiet, clear voice.

The green river of men and women flowed along the corridor, the slap of their sandals on the stones the only sound that filled the air. As the procession moved in unison to the great chamber at the end of the passage, the silence seemed to deepen. Lukas walked amongst them feeling a little self-conscious. It was not just because of his white garments, although those made him stand out amongst the silent walkers. It was his individuality, his unknowingness that made him self-conscious; he was not bound in the daily ritual of their lives and now he was aware of a certain clumsiness within himself, a need to concentrate upon the actions of others so he did not mar the harmony of the occasion. In his self-absorption it was a few moments before he realised that Naos was smiling at him and that indeed all faces were turned towards him with the same loving concern. Gratitude overwhelmed him; he could relax and be a part of the worship without worrying. As the singing began he opened his mouth and found the words escaping from his lips, and a peace so profound stole over him that his thoughts dissolved into a calm that was beyond any individual state, but part of a united meditation.

From the far side of the room Rosemary saw him, taller than anyone else there, his head tipped back a little, the black curls falling away from his fine, white face; even at a distance she could see his eyes brimming with liquid light. She marvelled at his beauty for a moment before she closed her eyes and opened her lips in song.

Sunlight flooding into the room through the light curtains woke Lukas out of a deep sleep. He opened his eyes to find his grandmother sitting on his bed gazing at him. She looked wonderfully fresh and young and the smile that lifted her mouth and flooded her eyes merged with the sun's rays and fell on his brow. She bent to drop a kiss on his forehead.

"You look very well rested this morning."

It was true, he had awoken full of energy and hope, and the pain in his hands was gone.

"I feel really good and ready to go whenever you feel strong enough."

"I'm ready now." He saw that she was fully dressed in her own clothes which had been freshly laundered, and that on the bedside chair his own clean garments were laid out, mended where they had been torn. "But before we leave, after you've had breakfast, Naos would like to talk to you."

He hesitated. "Why?"

"1 don't know, but you must go to see him; it's the very least you can do."

"Of course I'll go, I just wondered if he had a particular reason for wanting to see me."

The old lady looked at him for a moment.

"Only you can guess that, Lukas, but you can't fool a man like Naos."

He threw his arms around her neck and wept.

Naos sat in a room laced with sunlight, filled with the scent of the breeze that floated in through an open window, a room full of books and sacred pictures and an untouchable accumulation of intense thought. He rose to greet Lukas, grasping his hands warmly.

"Ah, Lukas, how good of you to come. Sit here by the window and share this beautiful morning with me."

To his surprise Lukas saw that there was no sign of the forest from this side of the house. Instead, a large garden meandered outside with wide grassy slopes, banks of flowers and slender trees that bent their bodies in fluid greeting.

"The forest ends beyond your front door?"

Lukas's question was cautious and Naos looked at him a long time before answering.

"Indeed, no forest encroaches onto our land. If you go to the end of our garden you will see only fields sloping away in the distance."

"And a path?" The words were out before Lukas could find a more measured way of asking the question.

"You will find a natural path across the fields."

"Where does it lead?" whispered Lukas.

"Ah, that depends upon which way you go."

"That is no answer!" Lukas looked at the older man imploringly.

"Yet it is the only answer I can give, so do not look for any other." The two men sat in silence for some time whilst Lukas stared out of the window and Naos watched him with concern. "But Lukas, do not think of leaving us yet. This is why I wish to speak with you this morning. You arrived last night exhausted, your grandmother almost in a state of collapse, but it was the condition of your mind that worried me most, for I felt an urgency and fear upon you like a physical weight. I also sensed a great love and an immense yearning. I do not understand what these feelings mean, but I feel their danger, both to yourself and your grandmother, and to…" He hesitated.

"To?"

"To whoever or whatever is involved in your journey and beyond."

"Is that all you can see, can't you be more specific?" cried Lukas, but the other man shook his head sadly. "Don't look at me like that, Naos; I only long to search for something beyond all common goodness."

"Are you sure?" Naos was staring at him keenly, but Lukas was gazing out of the window again and did not seem to hear his question.

"Is there a lake near here, a large lake of glittering reflections, surrounded by hills, and beyond it towering mountains?"

"Perhaps. I have heard of some such water from rumours handed down through the fables of our people, but no-one here has ever seen it. So that is what you are searching for?"

Lukas would not meet his eyes and Naos leant across and placed his hands upon the rigid shoulders of the other man; Lukas's white face tautened under his scrutiny and Naos saw the tongue running across the dry lips as he struggled to find an answer.

"I'm looking for more than that, but until I find the lake my search is hopeless."

"Do not search for something you will never find – that way lies terrible grief and danger. Stay here with us a while and find peace at last."

"No!" The wild cry startled them both and Lukas raised his eyes in fear. "I can't stop searching; what you suggest would mean the end of everything. I can't stay and rest."

"At least leave your grandmother here with us; she cannot survive much longer on such a journey."

"If she would stay, then of course I'd leave her behind." Lukas hesitated as he struggled with his feelings. "But she would never agree to such a suggestion, even if we both begged her to do so. It's too late to turn back." There was a long pause. Lukas waited for Naos to speak, but he remained silent. "Will you bless our journey before we go?"

"I will bless you, my son, but I cannot bless something which fills me with foreboding."

They both knew that there was nothing more to be said. For a brief moment Naos laid his hand on Lukas's forehead.

"Thank you, Naos." Without another word the younger man turned to leave and, in a few moments, he was out of the warm building, away from the quiet green-robed men and women and into the garden where his grandmother awaited him, ready to continue their journey.

Naos watched them from the window and sighed deeply. He had seen the veil of secrecy in Lukas's eyes and it had disturbed and saddened him; he wished with all his heart he could have prevented him from leaving.

# Chapter 18

In the distance the town looked enticing. It had appeared as if by magic as they turned a corner, its buildings nestling by a river that wound around its edges in graceful curves.

At first the early morning sunshine had warmed their heads as they walked down the long, grassy slopes but, as the day progressed, the sun slipped away and left them travelling under an empty sky. In Lukas's rucksack were the remnants of their mid-day meal, food so lovingly provided by the community, and he felt optimistic, despite the words of Naos that still echoed in his mind.

"Why! What town can that be?" asked his grandmother, frowning in puzzlement as she gazed at the buildings spread out below.

"I don't know, it's strange. Still, if we go there, perhaps someone will know of the whereabouts of the lake." The old lady looked at him sternly.

"Lukas, you know we will never find the lake by asking others; we must search for it alone."

"You're right," he admitted reluctantly, "we'll skirt around its edges and go on into the country beyond. For the moment, it's the only thing we can do anyway; there's no other path but the one we're on."

It was true. On either side of them coarse bracken now covered the ground, difficult enough for Lukas to negotiate, but impossible for his grandmother, whereas the route they were following offered a clear and easy descent.

"There must be a way around the town somewhere; we'll find it when we get nearer."

The old lady nodded. How patient and dignified she looked, although the tiredness etched around her eyes worried him. What a quality of spirit and strength she had despite everything she had to endure.

It was growing colder and, with each step, the air grew sharper. As they dropped lower the bracken gave way to exposed stretches of cracked earth where a few straggling clumps of grass and wiry gorse bushes clung to the hard surface. Occasional deep holes pitted its crust and the whole area looked treacherous and forbidding. They were obviously drawing closer to civilisation, however, for a fence ran along either side of their pathway separating them from the inhospitable landscape, leading them clearly in the direction of the town.

"Why, that's odd," said Lukas after a silence that had lasted for some time as they concentrated on their descent, "from a distance the town looked really attractive but, as we draw closer, it's quite ugly." His grandmother said nothing and, turning to look at her, he saw that her face was grey and that she was breathing in shallow, rapid gasps. He chastised himself bitterly for his selfishness. "Oh, I'm sorry," he cried as he helped her sit on the ground, kneeling to place his jacket around her, taking the bottle of water from the rucksack, feeding her a little of the delicious bread baked early that morning at the community.

"It's so cold," she whispered, and indeed the sky now brooded metal grey as onto their faces fell the first flakes of snow. The wind was rising and Lukas could see the blizzard approaching, white particles swirling in faint misty shrouds. Even as they rested, the temperature was tumbling and he shivered as he hastily pulled the rucksack on to his back and lifted his grandmother into his arms.

"We'll have to head for the town and find shelter." He was shouting, trying to make himself heard above the wind. The blizzard had caught them, smothering them in seconds with its stinging flakes, and he was finding it difficult to stand.

Holding his grandmother tightly against his chest, Lukas staggered blindly in the direction of the buildings.

The men sat huddled close to the fire, sheltered a little from the storm by the parapets of the bridge. Dressed in identical suits of grey, hooded capes of black around their shoulders, no distinguishing features separated them from one another in the wintry night. Nothing stirred but the fire, or a boot as it stamped the ground, or a hand as it beat a frozen thigh. No voice but that of the wind was heard apart from the occasional cough or oath. At last one of the men rose, dark against the swirling snow, and stood peering across the bridge.

"Whatever are you doing?" muttered one of his companions. "Sit down again."

"Someone or something is coming across the bridge towards us."

Roars of laughter greeted his words but, as they died away, faint echoes hung in the air to mock them. Out of the night stepped a tall figure, taller by far than any of them. In his arms he carried a bundle which he held tightly against his breast. The men jumped to their feet.

"Where have you come from, stranger, and what do you want here?"

"Shelter," said Lukas, "I must find shelter for my grandmother." They saw then the nature of the bundle and relaxed a little, shrugging their shoulders.

"Go on into the town," said one, "and see what you can find."

They did not turn to look as the figure faded from view into the biting snow, but sat down once more in silence.

Lukas knocked frantically on the stout, oak door.

"Let me in, let me in! My grandmother's dying and I must

146

find shelter!"

The door stood impassive before him, whilst behind the windows of the house no shadows moved to open it and bid them enter. He had lost count of how many doors he had hammered upon, how many windows he had beaten, how often he had called aloud for help. At times he thought he saw a light through a half-open shutter or heard voices behind barred doors but, whenever he drew closer, the light disappeared or the noises ceased. He was sobbing with despair. If someone opened up the smallest crack he would force his way in, but what could he do against the impenetrable muteness of closed doors?

"Let us in, you murderers!" There was no response and the houses shrank further into the night, hunched against his feeble onslaught.

He no longer knew whether his grandmother was alive or dead. She had not stirred for a long time and he dare not look at her face. He stumbled on, begging aloud for help, ready to sink into the snow and close his eyes against the emptiness; it was only the limp bundle in his arms that kept him moving. When he saw the shape battling its way towards him he assumed at first that he was hallucinating and he took no notice, but lowered his head and forced his way onwards. The voice, when it spoke, made him cry out in fear but, as he peered into the darkness, he saw a young boy standing before him, fifteen or sixteen years old, dressed shabbily and shivering in the cold, an old blanket held around his shoulders by a pin, the shoes upon his feet more suited to a summer's day.

"I'm Jonquil. We heard your cries for help. We can offer you shelter, although it's probably not the kind of shelter you're looking for."

"Any shelter will do. Please take me quickly; my grandmother's dying."

Wordlessly he followed the child through the winding streets, concentrating all his effort upon not falling. He did not notice where they walked, but after a time a strong aroma drifted into his nostrils and, with each step, it became more pronounced, until he tried to breathe through his mouth to avoid the unpleasant stench.

"We're nearly there," said Jonquil as he led him down a small slope into a strange, flickering and shadowy twilight world. After a startled moment Lukas realised he had been led underneath the extension of a bridge; for all he knew it could be the bridge he had crossed earlier. Moisture ran down the walls, but they were out of the merciless blizzard and here, in this strange place, welcome and help awaited them.

How many fires burnt there, in roughly-made brick containers, in rusty braziers, it was impossible to tell, but their joint flames threw hesitant light and ghostly shadows and provided spots of warmth beneath the dank roof. Huddled around the fires were spectres of the night, some curled up in sleep, some wakeful, following Lukas's tentative journey into their midst with patient eyes. It was from these people that the smell came, from unwashed bodies and the decay of poverty but, as Lukas followed Jonquil past the groups of watchers, they smiled at him in encouragement.

"This is my family." Jonquil pointed to a corner where a fire crackled cheerfully and young and old gathered around its warmth. "I've found them, Father," he said to a middle-aged man with merry eyes, dressed like everyone else in ragged clothes.

"Good boy, Jonquil. Quick everyone!" The man took Lukas's grandmother into his arms, then laid her gently on a pile of sacking by the fire. Two of the women undressed her with great care and wrapped her in old blankets, then one of them held some hot, pungent smelling liquid to the old woman's lips, whilst two smaller children rubbed her hands and crooned comfort to her. A small crowd gathered quickly round them offering advice and assistance. After a while the eyes of his grandmother opened a little and she spluttered as the liquid coursed down her throat.

"She's alive!" Lukas threw himself to his knees beside her, covering her face with tears and kisses. His grandmother smiled weakly at him but she did not speak.

"Come." Gently, Jonquil's father took Lukas by the arm and helped him to his feet. "Your grandmother will be alright now. My wife will look after her; she'll soon fall into a healing sleep. You need something as well," and he handed Lukas a bowl of steaming liquid, drawing him closer to the fire. "Drink that, and then you can take off those sodden clothes and we'll give you something dry to wear."

For a while Lukas could only express his gratitude by obeying; he stood by the flames sipping the boiling broth, feeling the warmth flow back into his body. But a little later, when he was changed into the dry rags and his own clothes hung by the fire, when his grandmother slept peacefully, cocooned in the old blankets so that only her face was exposed to the air, he turned to Jonquil's father to ask the question that had been hovering on his lips for some time.

"How did you know I needed help? You couldn't possibly have heard my cries from here."

The other man took a stick and stirred some burning twigs. The younger children slept, lying on the floor upon a pile of old cloth, sharing a thin blanket, whilst Jonquil sat with his mother chatting quietly. The others had dispersed reluctantly to their own fires, ready to return if needed.

"There are different ways of hearing cries for help, my friend. It's enough that you were heard and that your call was answered."

Lukas persisted. "But I shouted in the street and hammered

149

on a hundred doors. No-one answered, yet surely they knew I was there; I don't understand."

"Ah." Jonquil's father looked at him quizzically. "Why do you have to understand?"

Lukas laughed, the first laugh he had uttered for a long time.

"You're not the only person to ask me that question." He leant forward and placed his own white, slim hand on the rough and dirty hand of his companion. "Thank you." The other man shook his head and smiled.

"No more talking now, it's time for some sleep; I'll fetch you a blanket."

Lukas felt an overwhelming sense of relief: he was exhausted and hardly knew how to find the energy to lie down.

All around him the many fires burned, and shadows danced upon the ground and walls, but Lukas was asleep in seconds and saw no more that night.

The whole cavernous shelter was sleeping apart from one sentinel by each fire guarding the precious flames. Lukas was sunk in a slumber so profound that he did not hear the sound of logs being thrown upon the blaze, or the whisper of falling ash, or the voices of the watchers as they called softly to one another throughout the night. And neither he nor anyone else was aware of a form that stole into the breathing shelter for a while, gliding unseen across the dark floor to where he lay, to gaze intently at his unconscious face before slipping out silently once more into the treacherous night.

Lukas woke slowly to the realisation that something was different. His grandmother was already up, sitting patiently on a piece of wood, and Jonquil knelt beside her turning over the last few embers of the fire. Otherwise, the whole shelter was deserted and all the other fires of the night before were extinguished.

"Where is everyone?" Lukas whispered, but his grandmother put a finger to her lips and Jonquil stirred uneasily.

"They're gone and we have to leave immediately. Jonquil is waiting to lead us through the town to the path on the other side."

Lukas knew it was useless to ask further questions. Something strange must have happened to empty the shelter of all its inhabitants, but at least the boy remained to help them find their way out of this wretched town. Rapidly, he pulled on his dry clothes and within minutes he was ready, pausing only briefly to drink from the cup his grandmother gave him. Jonquil was standing now, tapping his feet anxiously on the ground. Lukas picked up his rucksack and took the arm of the old lady.

"Are you alright to move on again so quickly?" he asked with concern, looking at her tired face. Any other person of her age would have died long ago, or given up completely; it was extraordinary how she survived and retained her determination and spirit.

"I've no choice, but I want to go. There's no place for us here and I believe that it isn't safe for us to stay. We'll travel slowly."

He had to be satisfied with her answer although he still felt very uneasy; they would have to rest along the way and he would carry her as much as he could. He turned to Jonquil.

"We're ready."

He longed to ask the boy what had happened to his family, to send his thanks to them, but he knew that Jonquil did not want to talk.

In the morning light the town had lost its derelict

appearance. To his relief and surprise Lukas saw that the snow had melted, and now the windows of the houses were flung wide to the air and the doors were fully open. Furthermore, the streets were no longer deserted, but filled with people hurrying along, so that the noise of their clattering footsteps beat a tattoo upon the stones. Lukas gazed in astonishment: these were not their companions of the night, but well-dressed, prosperous citizens.

"Everyone seems to be in a great hurry," muttered Lukas to his grandmother. "Wherever can they all be rushing to so early in the morning?"

The old lady shook her head, but before she could reply the striking of a clock immediately above them drowned out the possibility of speaking and, even as they looked up in surprise, the sound of other clocks across the town added their voices to the clamour, rising in urgency and vibration until the very buildings trembled. What time they were striking it was impossible to tell; indeed it seemed the hour they boomed out was unending, spun beyond measure, for the clanging notes struck on and on, past twelve, past twelve hundred, striking an hour that had not yet come and could not exist. At the sound of the first clock the citizens started in agitation, then strode faster along the street in a mounting crescendo of motion.

Lukas and his grandmother held their hands to their ears and gazed around in amazement.

"I don't think the townspeople can see us," thought Lukas. "They're staring straight ahead as if at something a great distance away, but we're invisible to them. Whoever are they and what on earth are they doing?"

In front of them he could see Jonquil darting in and out amongst the crowd. Lukas grasped his grandmother's hand more firmly and tried to support her as best he could, for they must not lose sight of the boy. As quickly as it had started the cry of the clocks ceased but, as the last note shivered into silence, Lukas became aware of an undercurrent of sound, and gradually he realised that the people walking quickly past were speaking to themselves.

"Hurry, hurry!"

The words were a chanted incantation repeated endlessly, so that he found the rhythm of their voices beating in his brain and he had to make a determined effort not to increase his own pace and risk harming his grandmother. The blood seemed to pump in his head in time with the chanting; he thought of Naos's quiet words of warning and the calm of that sanctuary and longed, for a moment, to retrace his steps.

Jonquil had stopped and was beckoning to them urgently, and a moment later they turned into a quiet side street, hidden from the frenzied activity of the main thoroughfare. Here they walked on deserted pavements, into shaded alleyways, until suddenly they were out in the open once more where only a few houses straggled at the edge of the town. In the distance they could see the people still hastening along and, across the air, their chanting could still be heard faintly on the breeze.

Lukas and his grandmother stared after the vanishing citizens for a few moments and then turned away. The people were disappearing and they would never know who they were.

"This is your path." Jonquil pointed to the ribbon of grass that wound along beside the river and then melted into the distance. Lukas tightened his grip on his grandmother's hand.

"It looks an easy path. We'll go slowly, there's no hurry at all."

For a moment they both gazed at the faint horizon, at the curling river and the path that meandered by its side, then they turned to say farewell to Jonquil. Where he had placed his feet upon the grass not even the smallest indentation touched the green earth. He was gone and they were alone once more.

## Chapter 19

Lukas had not forgotten Claire and the children. They were continually in his heart as he travelled and, when he thought of their faces, they were smiling and Claire had the old, open look of long ago.

"When I reach the wall," he said to his grandmother, "and discover what the boy from the other side was trying to show me, then at last I'll understand what I've been looking for all this time and will be able to explain my behaviour to Claire."

They were sitting by the river, close to the reeds where the bank sloped down to the water's edge. They had eaten a little more of the bread and drunk the last of the water from the bottle, but Lukas felt confident that they would be able to replenish their supply at a stream along the way. All morning they had walked beneath clouds that hovered silver-grey against a pale canvas. His grandmother seemed almost completely refreshed and moved without difficulty along the smooth, grassy path.

"How do you know that the boy was trying to show you something? Perhaps he wanted to find out something from you; perhaps he was searching for something he thought you could give him."

"No, no, what have I to show anyone? The call I heard is for me to go to the other side of the wall, for the boy who's now a man couldn't possibly wish to cross over here. His face shone with a goodness I've never seen before. I think the country he comes from is like nothing we could imagine."

"The wall, the wall, only you have seen it, Lukas, and I'm afraid it's not to be found again. We may find the lake but I sense that will be the end of our journey."

"No!" He jumped to his feet in agitation. "Don't lose faith now when we've come so far."

She looked at him towering over her, his back to the river. He spoke of the appearance of the other boy, but surely no-one could surpass the compelling beauty of her grandson. Even in the short time they had been gone from home his black curls seemed to have grown and tumbled around his white face, emphasizing the startling green of his eyes.

"I'm not losing faith. I'll stay with you until you find what you're looking for."

He smiled at her with such grateful love that she felt tears stinging her eyes. She pointed to the way ahead.

"Look, the path carries on by the water and the weather's good. I'm sure we're getting nearer to the lake. Let's sleep for a while before we go any further."

He did not say what was constantly on his mind: how was it that, when he discovered the wall as a boy, he and his grandmother had found the lake during a morning's walk, yet now they had already spent several nights away from home and there was still no sign of it?

"Sleep awhile," he said, and so they lay down to rest, whilst the river flowed swiftly past them and the clouds dipped and parted above their heads.

There was sand on his lips, in his eyes, and the taste of grit was on his tongue as he choked for breath. It stretched in all directions, in golden ridges, whilst the bonfire of the sky dripped waxen. He leapt to his feet searching desperately for the cool grass, the clear river, but it was hopeless, for the arid air could never have tasted water. His grandmother still slept, but her lips were swollen and cracked and her skin blistering.

"Oh," moaned Lukas, "why did I go to sleep and not keep

watch?" He opened and closed his eyes rapidly trying to dispel the nightmare but, whichever way he looked, the sand shimmered and shifted, and in all that barren landscape the only moisture was the tears of his despair. "Grandmother, wake up, something has happened whilst we slept and we're in a desert being burnt by the sun even as I speak! We must move quickly."

The old lady was fully awake within seconds; she looked around at the endless expanse of desert and up at the sun which pinpointed its rays onto her scorched and withered face.

"Water," she whispered but, even as he reached for the bottle, he remembered.

"I forgot to fill the bottle!"

She had shrunk into an ageless knot of pain. He helped her to her feet and they stood on the sand with their arms about each other, paralysed by dismay.

"It can't be," whispered his grandmother, "not now," and she turned her back and began to shuffle slowly away. With a shudder Lukas followed, the sweat pouring down his face and back whilst the sun cut through his flesh. He tried to run his tongue over his swollen lips but it seemed rooted in his mouth, painfully parched in a prison of teeth and gums. He had no strength left and was ready to fall to the ground and stretch out his body on the sand in surrender, but he could not abandon his grandmother. She continued to move forward, stepping out of her pain and despair as if shedding unwanted clothing, and she never looked back or stumbled, as the sand murmured under her footprints and the hot breeze lifted her white hair. After what felt like hours he could tolerate it no longer

"We're going to die here in this hell. There's no point in walking any further." He was almost screaming.

She didn't turn or reply, but put one foot in front of another and he had no choice but to follow. Just when he thought he would have to lie down and give up, she pointed ahead.

"See, Lukas!"

He peered intently and saw only the endless desert of certain death.

"I can't see anything but sand."

"Look again, look, there's water ahead."

"No!" The cry exploded from his swollen and blistered lips. "It's a mirage, everything is a mirage! There's nothing but desert."

She took no notice of him, walking on as if he had not spoken. He longed to look back, to see if any shadow glided behind them, but he dare not. He did not know how long they walked, for he staggered like a man crazed, holding the hand of his grandmother as if he were a child again.

"Do you hear now," she cried, "can you see?" and in his exhilaration he ran past her towards the distant waves which were breaking onto the shore.

"Do you remember that time I took you to the sea when you were a young boy? It was the same every day. We left the house to walk to the beach and every day you were convinced that the sea wouldn't be there. You were always surprised and thrilled when we turned the last corner and saw the water."

"I was always a doubter, but how could we have expected to see an ocean at the edge of this desert?"

"Nothing is impossible on this journey, Lukas."

"You're right. I never seem to learn, always taking things at face value." His grandmother said nothing.

In the distance they could see cranes and the funnels of great ships. They linked arms and walked until they reached the quayside, joining crowds of people moving in the same direction. Their target rose majestically out of the water, its white hull gleaming.

"Where is this ship going?" Lukas asked a man about to climb up the gangway.

"Don't you know?" He looked at Lukas curiously, his eyes resting for a moment on the white face before shrugging his shoulders and turning away.

"Look at the horizon, Lukas," said his grandmother, "it's all misted with pinks and mauves. The ship must be going in that direction, towards the colours of the flowers of the valley."

He needed no second bidding.

"Where do I pay?" he asked a crew member on the quayside, although even as he spoke he remembered he had no money.

"Later, you pay later, there's no time now."

It was strangely quiet on the decks. Lukas had expected to find it crowded, but the promenades were empty and the echoing boards held nothing but their own footsteps.

"There must be a way into the ship," breathed Lukas as he searched up and down the decks for a door. Through the glass he could see people walking around, but they were like shadows in a silent film and he did not even attempt to attract their attention. The ship was moving, steaming away from the land out into the open sea.

"What shall we do?" The old lady looked tired again and he realised they had still not drunk anything.

"We'll find a sheltered spot and rest, and later I'll look for a way inside." Lukas tried to sound more positive than he felt. He found a nook in the stern and made her as comfortable as possible, then filled the water bottle from a barrel close by and helped her to drink before gulping some of the liquid himself. He took a shawl from the rucksack and wrapped it around the old lady's shoulders, for the breeze was suddenly much cooler. No-one came near them and no sound could be heard but the throb of the engines and the cry of the gulls as they followed the ship. They were far out into the ocean now and, whilst the waves raced along beside them, the horizon flamed crimson with the sun sitting upon the edge of the sea, dappling its long legs in the glistening water.

The dreadful wailing of the ship's siren woke them from a cold, cramped sleep. Nothing could be seen in the darkness.

"What's happening?" cried grandmother.

"She's going down!" Lukas staggered to his feet, realising to his horror that the ship was already listing and the deck would soon be covered by water. "Help! Don't leave us behind, where are the lifeboats?"

His grandmother stood by his side, old beyond belief in the clashing night and stricken air. There was the sound of splintering wood as the ship shuddered lower. Lukas held the old lady tightly around the waist and, clinging to the railing with his spare hand, pulled them both along the deck. The sea sucked close beside them. He looked around desperately for some crew members, their fellow passengers, but no-one was to be seen. He clutched his grandmother closer.

"We're going to jump clear of the ship; keep your arms tight around my neck!"

"It's no good," she moaned, but she clung to him as he leapt, and he flung back his head as they hit the water, so that his eyes flamed with the stars, whilst the ship groaned and plunged deeper into the waves.

They were in a small boat, snatched from the sea by unseen hands. In the darkness they could only make out the shadowy silhouettes of their rescuers, but their voices could be heard clearly.

"Where are we?"

"Where are the others?"

"We're going to die."

"Sit still!"

"There's nothing we can do."

"Nothing," thought Lukas as he slipped into unconsciousness beside the lifeless form of his grandmother.

The stench was unendurable. They held their hands across their mouths, their noses, but the foul odour invaded their senses with its obscene, clinging rankness. Lukas felt the bile rising to his mouth, the taste mixing with the fetid smell, until he thought his very flesh must rot and grow sour.

They were becalmed and marooned in a vast sea of mud. Black, gleaming, shifting in belching gulps under the base of the small boat, its slime beckoned, enticing them to escape, for beyond it they could see land, richly green and verdant, enchanting in its contrasting loveliness.

Early light had come and Lukas now saw his companions clearly for the first time: two middle-aged men, an older man with a swarthy face dressed in a bedraggled uniform, and a woman of indefinite years who clutched a small packet to her breast as if her life depended upon its protection.

"Where are we?" cried Lukas, speaking through clenched teeth as the terrible stink drew vomit to his mouth.

"Stuck," wailed the woman, "we must get away."

"Impossible, we'll drown in the mud." But no-one was listening and, to his dismay, Lukas saw that they were preparing to step from the boat.

"You can't stop them, Lukas." His grandmother was awake, gazing with pity on the scene.

"Perhaps they're right; if we stay here we'll die as well, but more slowly."

"No, we must wait here."

"Don't go," implored Lukas as the woman crawled over the side of the boat. She took no notice, sliding onto the mud

161

on her stomach so that it squelched between her splayed fingers and pouted its thick lips against her thighs until she took on the appearance of some strange creature that had emerged from the very womb of the stinking estuary bed. Yet she was moving quickly over the surface, heading for the dry land in the distance.

"She's making progress!" cried one of the middle-aged men and, a moment later, he too was over the side on his belly, swimming on a surface that sunk into his pores, trickling into his nostrils and mouth. Soon only Lukas and his grandmother were left in the boat, watching with ever increasing horror as the figures became embalmed in the mud, sinking lower with each stroke, until they seemed a very part of the fermenting surface and were lost from sight.

# Chapter 20

Solan watched the boat as it drifted towards her. She had been observing it for some time since it had floated across the wide estuary into her view, moving with the waters that flowed with the incoming tide. She was curious because the boat appeared to be empty. No sail billowed in the wind, no oars hung from its side, yet it must have travelled from the open sea to this place, moving as if it knew its destination.

Solan was at that stage between girlhood and womanhood, still a child in many ways, yet her face was touched with an approaching grace that rendered her gangling body unimportant. She had not seen another living soul for a very long time so, when the boat first appeared, a great sense of anticipation mixed with fear made her cry aloud and run along the cliff side, never losing sight of the approaching craft as it drew nearer. She had raced to the sandy shoreline of the estuary until she was forced to climb higher by the steep rocks that jutted out at the far end of the broad expanse of water. Then she climbed quickly into the woods above, sprinting through the familiar trees until she could drop down once more to the water which had now narrowed into a gently flowing river.

She waited patiently. It came at last, and only then was she certain that the boat drifted alone, navigated merely by the scurrying wind and the tide. As she gazed the bow swung towards her, eerie in its empty momentum, and travelled across the current until its nose nudged the shore where she waited breathlessly.

It was not unoccupied as she had thought, but the deathly cradle for two people who lay across the bottom. The woman was tiny, delicate-featured, white hair loose around her face. It was impossible to guess her age: there was something youthful in her appearance yet, when the girl looked more closely, the skull could have been dug from an ancient tomb. The man seemed younger, but the dreadful pallor of his face made it difficult to know. Solan caught hold of the boat's bow and pulled it a little way onto the shingle, then leant over, pressing her ear against the chest of the dark stranger.

He lived. His heart beat strongly and, even as she drew back to gaze once more at the white face, Lukas opened his eyes and the girl gasped at the contrast of his green eyes against the white skin.

"For God's sake, who are you?" Lukas struggled to sit up, then looked in despair at the motionless form of his grandmother.

"I'm Solan. I saw your boat floating across the estuary. Where have you come from? What's happened to you?" Lukas did not answer her questions.

"Please help me to lift my grandmother and lie her over there. I'm afraid that she's… "

"Forgive me, I wasn't thinking," cried Solan. They lifted the old woman and carried her to the soft grass where Solan knelt by her side and rubbed the old lady's hands and stroked her brow. After a while she turned to smile at Lukas.

"She's sleeping, that's all. She'll wake in a moment."

"Are you really sure?"

The girl laughed.

"Let her come to in her own time; we mustn't startle her." She looked back to the boat and then at Lukas and the dishevelled state of his clothes. "Have you no supplies, nothing?"

"Everything has been lost on the journey. We've nothing at all." He leant over the old lady and stroked her brow and, as he did so, the girl was gone, running up the bank back into the woods. "Stop!" It was no good; the only answer was the snapping of twigs in the distance. He sighed; she had obviously taken fright and run off to her people. It was to be hoped they were friendly.

His grandmother was stirring, opening her eyes.

"Where are we? I must have slept – I'm feeling much better."

"We're safe. You've been sleeping a long time. Just lie quietly now."

What could account for her strange resilience, her ability to recover from the most gruelling ordeals, when a much younger person would have been defeated long ago? Nothing made sense on this strange and tortuous journey. He rocked her in his arms and felt the warmth of the sun on his head and heard the sound of birdsong in his ears. It was so peaceful he felt as if he could rest here for ever, and he didn't move until he heard the crackling of twigs from the woodland again and Solan was there before him. She smiled shyly, offering gifts of wild berries and honey, oddly shaped biscuits and water in rough, earthenware cups.

"This is all I have at the moment, but please take it; you must be so hungry and thirsty." The simple food tasted like nectar and, even as the girl watched over them, Lukas felt his strength returning.

"Thank you, thank you," they said again and again, whilst she shook her head laughing and glowed with their gratitude.

Now at last he could begin to take notice of their surroundings. The river was crystal clear, running between green banks and willowy trees. It was all calm and peace. There was not a building in sight, nor any sign of human habitation.

"Where are your parents, Solan?" Lukas asked. "Where are your people?"

"I've no-one, I'm alone here. It's been just me since my father died."

"How can a girl like you survive alone? Isn't there a village near here, no town where you could get help?"

Solan looked at him through grave eyes and stepped back a little.

"There's nothing."

"But when your father was alive, he must have taken you to school, to some kind of community? Haven't you any other relatives, no-one at all to care for you?" Solan shook her head slowly.

"You don't seem to understand. I knew my father had to die. I'm not lonely, only alone. You needn't worry about me."

He wasn't convinced by her words; there was something vulnerable about her that made him long to gather her close and keep her safe. Perhaps it was the thought of his own daughter, far away. His grandmother was sitting on the grass gazing across the river. She had been listening to the conversation intently but had said nothing, and the expression in her eyes was unfathomable. Now she turned to the girl and touched her arm gently.

"We've no right to question Solan, to try to make her give us some answers," she said, and the girl smiled gratefully.

"There's no way you could, however much I might grow to want it."

Lukas knew that he could pursue the subject no further, although he felt a sadness gathering in his chest.

"Tell me about your journey. Maybe I can help you."

He felt a sudden rush of blood to his face as new possibilities came into his mind.

"I believe you could help us if you wished."

"I don't always know what to do. My father taught me many things before he died and one was that humans can

166

choose the way they travel. That's why I'm alone now. Tell me what you're looking for."

"We're searching for a lake, a vast lake, that lies in a valley covered in flowers, and behind it the hills lead on up towards the mountains beyond."

"I know the lake. It's only half a day's journey from here; I can lead you there."

Lukas buried his face in his hands, but his grandmother took the girl's hands into her own, drawing her near so she could look fully at her face.

"Is there anything near the lake, anything unusual, anything at all that could have been built a long time ago?"

Solan was startled. "What sort of thing do you mean?"

"If there was something there you would have seen it."

"There's nothing there. Nothing has ever been built there."

"Do you hear what Solan says, Lukas?"

He shook his head and turned to the girl.

"Will you lead us to the lake, Solan?"

"I'll take you to the valley of flowers, and then you must walk across on your own. I can't go any further with you."

"Is it really that simple," whispered Lukas, "after everything, to be led there beneath a sunny sky across a land that holds no terrors?"

He did not see the tremor that ran through the slender form of the girl, nor notice the way she lowered her eyes to the ground and gave no answer.

Lukas did not want the walk to come to an end. He felt as if they had been transported to a land of eternal beauty as Solan guided them through the woods and by the side of a small tributary of the river that gurgled in tune with the day. They moved in a steady rhythm along the grassy tracks without speaking, for the air suffused their minds with blues and greens and yellow sunlight, and they were wrapped in a multi-coloured breeze that mingled its breath with theirs and made them silent.

At last Lukas paused, throwing back his head and inhaling deeply.

"Do you smell it, the scent of a million flowers?"

Solan turned to him. "We're nearly at the valley."

"Let's hurry!" urged Lukas.

"No." Solan spoke softly, but her words were adamant. "There's no need to hurry. We must go steadily for your grandmother's sake."

"You've more sense than I have." Lukas looked rueful. "Let's rest for a while before we carry on."

Only now he realised that, in his eagerness to press forward, he had not made sure often enough that his grandmother was not becoming too tired, but she smiled at him.

"Keep going, I'm perfectly alright," she said, and he was pleased to believe her.

They carried on walking for some time, speaking little as they travelled. Solan held the old lady's hand and Lukas sensed that the girl could have walked for ever in that companionable silence. Suddenly, however, she paused and pointed to a ridge a little way ahead.

"There."

In his excitement Lukas ran ahead, leaping over the grass like a boy, whilst the others followed slowly behind. At last the three of them stood together looking down at the sight before them, at the medley of colours, the bursting beauty, the pungent profusion of the valley of flowers. Lukas fell to his knees, holding out his arms as he shouted aloud his ecstasy and the tears that flooded his eyes shimmered like the vast expanse of water beyond the end of the valley. His grandmother placed her hand upon his head, trembling at the vista which had been buried in her memory for thirty years.

Solan stood behind them waiting to say farewell. She knew that for the moment they had forgotten her, and she made no move until at last Lukas wiped his eyes and jumped to his feet.

"Why, Solan, I'm sorry. How can we ever thank you? Now we're here, you must come with us to the lake." The girl shook her fair head.

"I can't go any further."

"You told us yourself there is no-one to go back to," Lukas pleaded. "Stay with us and let us look after you. We can't leave you here."

Solan shook her head again.

"Please don't try to persuade me, I can't go with you." She turned to the old lady who stood watching silently. "I must say goodbye."

His grandmother held out her arms and the young girl ran into them.

"Bless you," whispered the old lady.

"I'll never forget you. Please take great care as you cross the valley."

They stepped apart at last and Solan turned to where Lukas's silent form threw a shadow across the grass.

"Goodbye, Lukas." They looked at each other, the man and the girl, and longed for the final parting to be over, to fade into the past, to release them from its pain. They grasped hands for a moment before Lukas bent and kissed her on the brow.

"Thank you, Solan. Goodbye."

"Goodbye!"

The young cry echoed all around them as the slight figure shrank into the distance and their own shouts mingled with hers until at last the space between them buried the sounds.

Lukas led the way across the valley of flowers. He walked

with urgent strides, never looking to where his feet bruised the delicate heads, for his whole concentration was on the water that drew closer with each step. His grandmother, however, was increasingly distracted as she followed, and she kept on glancing around and listening intently as she went. Her sense of well-being and hopefulness had vanished and the old fear returned. The presence was back; she felt it in the very air and in the muted tones of the wind, whilst the sweet-smelling flowers were, in their very kaleidoscope of colours, a camouflage for anything that wished to creep unseen upon the ground. More than once she paused, straining her ears: it was there for a moment, a slight rustling, as if some object had slithered through dead leaves.

"Lukas," she whispered, but he seemed quite unaware of anything unusual and the question fell back into her throat. She would not worry him now when he was so full of joy and excitement.

After a while, she knew that she would not be able to go on much further for, despite her great desire to keep moving, she found her steps faltering and her breath coming in short gasps. She opened her mouth to call out to Lukas, trying to force her tongue to utter the cry for help but, even as she struggled, the rustling sound was at her very feet and the flowers parted as the form glided towards her, its eyes fixed on her shaking body.

"Lukas!" The pain seared through her arm and he turned at last, running to catch her as she fell.

"Grandmother, what is it, what's happened?" He carried her the short distance to where the grasses touched the clear water, but she made no answer, and he laid her on the ground and dipped the end of his shirt into the lake, bathing her forehead until she opened her eyes at last.

"You must say goodbye to me too, Lukas. I told you I felt

my journey would end at the lake."

"No, no, I won't let you go, you can't leave me now!"

"My strength's been taken, I've only a little time."

"Don't say that! You must stay, you will be well again."

"You must listen to me, Lukas." Although she was growing weaker she struggled to speak. "Go no further. You must return to Claire and the children. Take the path back to Solan; I'm sure she will guide you. There's great danger, not just for you but for…"

Lukas kissed the face again and again, the gentle face that shrivelled into age even as, for a moment, the youthful glow of approaching death smoothed the skin.

"Don't worry, Grandmother, I won't go any further. I'll go back and find Solan."

All around the beauty breathed unchanged. In their profusion of colours the flowers spread across the valley and, beyond the water, the mountains soared into the sky. Lukas did not notice. He saw nothing but his grandmother's dead face and knew nothing but that she was gone and he was alone without her.

For a long time he knelt beside her, quite unaware of his surroundings, until the earth was saturated with his tears and his head beat with grief. He could not bear to bury her and yet he could not leave her lying alone in that deserted place. At last he moved and, after searching for a while, he found a shallow hole in the grass where the ground was soft and pliable and here, through endless emptiness, he dug until his hands were raw and the old wounds seeped a little blood.

She lay in the earth like a child and he crossed her hands on her breast and smoothed her hair around her face and kissed again and again the quiet brow, and he called and called to her as he covered her with the earth and placed flowers over the mound, and he cried her name again and again as he stood at the water's edge and gazed across to the mountains.

At last he lowered his head, and could see a faint reflection of himself in the water, slightly distorted by the ripples on the surface. He looked away.

"Forgive me," he whispered. For he knew that he would journey on and that his last words to his grandmother had slipped over his tongue in comforting deception, and now he would never know if she had realised that the only lie he had ever told her had been uttered when that lie could never be undone.

The path towards the mountains stretched before him. He had followed the same route as thirty years ago, along the lakeside, branching off after a while in the direction of the peaks. Every now and then he rubbed his hands together where the old wounds throbbed incessantly; he must have hurt himself digging the grave, for the skin felt rough to the touch, almost jagged. The wall must be there somewhere, and he waited minute by minute for the sun to disappear as it had done before, gazing ahead desperately, searching for the shadow which would throw its dark mantle over him. The grasses grew spikier and scattered rocks lay around him, but still the light beat on his head and no stony barrier rose before him with its promise of another world.

"Where are you?" he shouted, stopping at last in despair, the sweat knotting his black curls and his eyes flashing with anger.

He heard the sound then, a rustling as the form came towards him, the small eyes staring into the green fire of Lukas's disgust. The stick was in his hand before he knew he had bent to grasp it. His arm swung back as he lifted it high, bringing it down even as the creature reared before him. Again and again he smashed the pulping head, screaming his rage and pain until he could no longer see the eyes, until the form was quite motionless in the dust.

Then at last the heat of the sun was quenched and the shadow sprang out of the ground, throwing him into the shade. Slowly he dropped the stick to the ground, not noticing in his rapture the empty spot where the creature had lain. He saw only the wall, and stone upon stone climbing up to a summit that had filled his sleeping and his waking thoughts for thirty years.

# Chapter 21

For Nathan, the fourth morning since the departure of his father had dawned poignantly beautiful. Although every day unfolded with consistent grace, to the boy this particular morning glimmered with a special quality so that, although the absence of Galen tugged at his heart, he could not help but rejoice at the splendour.

He was returning from the food gathering and, in his basket, he carried the light but delicious fare for the day's meals. He had been each morning since Galen's departure to collect the supplies, and the greetings from friends and Counsellors, relatives and school companions, had always been warm and loving. Yet Nathan sensed their fleeting glances to see if Galen followed close behind, and saw the brief shadowing on their faces when they realised he was not there. Each look, however quickly suppressed, sharpened his own sense of loss.

The boy walked with his uncles, some of his older cousins, his neighbours, enjoying the comfort of their conversation and feeling the support of their love.

"We will see you very shortly, Nathan," they said as they parted and he nodded, smiling. He walked home alone and, as he approached the house, he began to run. He flung the door wide open, calling aloud to his mother and sister.

"Come quickly and smell the morning! Surely, oh surely father will return today."

Anna glided softly from her room and joined the eager boy, placing her hands on his shoulders and breathing deeply as air flooded in through the open door. But she did not reply to Nathan's question, only gently squeezed his tense shoulders before she exchanged greetings with him.

Before he could ask her again, Rachel's voice rang through the house so that the unuttered answer hung between them like a watching cloud.

The great Centre of Worship shimmered with light as the people sang the Song of Awakening. All eyes were lifted to where the roof fell away into impenetrable brightness, whilst outside the whole place lay silent in the early sunshine, awaiting the moment when the doors would open and the people come out.

They sang this morning with a greater voice and an even fuller harmony than usual. The building soared with their song and shone with the glow of their upturned faces as the Counsellors led them through the timeless ritual. But at the end of the Celebration, instead of the usual loving dismissal, one of the Counsellors stepped forward and held out his arms as a sign that he wished to speak. It was Hedron.

"My dear friends, I know that we are all ready to return to our homes in order to refresh ourselves before we begin our daily work. However, at a gathering of the Counsellors last night, we decided that we must take the unknown step of breaking into our rhythm in order to safeguard it."

The people listened and waited to know what they must do. Only Anna stirred slightly as Hedron spoke.

"We are all aware that one of our people has set out upon a solitary and undisclosed journey. Since the early beginnings, when Jedra came back with his message, no-one has journeyed across the great plain alone. Galen has been gone three days and three nights and still there is no sign of his returning. We know that he parted from his wife beneath the arms of the mighty Tree. We are going to walk there this morning and strive to feel his presence and so bring him home. If any of you wish to journey with us, we shall be glad of your loving support."

There was a murmur amongst the people, and those standing closest to Anna, Nathan and Rachel showed their sympathy in their faces. Yet Anna stared only at Hedron. She knew of the planned journey to the plain, for the Counsellors had sent for her the previous evening and told her of their concern. They had asked if she felt there was anything she could tell them.

"I feel sure Galen's grandmother has a sense of what is happening to him but she will not speak at all. Since he left she has sat in her chair by the window and not spoken a word, although the family has tried to communicate with her."

"The old one loves her grandson with a deep heart," one of the younger Counsellors said gently.

"Not as much as I!" cried Anna involuntarily, and gasped as she realised what she had said.

"Ah, Anna," murmured Hedron.

The Counsellors were waiting. They would not force or hurry her, but they would not speak again until she had spoken. Anna stood before them a long time before she found the words were upon her tongue.

"I gave Galen an apple to take with him on his journey to remind him of all that he held dear. But he knew he must not eat it, that he must never even hold it near his lips. He carried it with him in his haversack, wrapped in a cloth."

It was one of the female Counsellors who finally broke the silence.

"But, Anna, with the apple removed from its source, how can Galen have a sense of the roots of the Tree and of the branches that shelter the fruit through all the days and nights of its existence?"

"It was foolish of me. For a few moments I lost sight of all I had been taught. My only concern was to link Galen to me as he walked away towards the mountains. That was wrong of me, but he will not eat of the apple, I know he will never do that."

No one spoke. They looked at her and saw there the desire to succour and hold her husband that had led her to touch the forbidden fruit. At last Hedron spoke.

"We know that we must not seek the knowledge that the Tree shelters us from. We pray with all our strength that Galen will not taste the fruit but, having taken it from its living source, we cannot say what the outcome will be. Such a thing has never happened amongst our people. It is as Jedra warned us."

"But the creature, there was no sign of the creature!" They did not answer and she gazed at the circle of quiet faces imploringly. "I said goodbye to him under the Tree," she wept, "and, since that moment, have lived only for his return."

"We will journey together to the great plain tomorrow morning after the Celebration of Awakening," said Hedron, "and listen again to the song of the River and stand beneath the Tree, and we will call with a loud voice to Galen and pray that he will hear and so return to his people, the apple whole within the napkin, ready to be restored to its rightful home."

Anna wept again as she thought of the boy with the golden, tumbling curls who had stood amongst their people as a child with all the marks of a Counsellor upon his young brow.

"I should have listened to you, but I thought I knew."

"Ah." The sigh could have come from any mouth.

The Counsellors led the way down the valley and onto the vast plain. The people flowed behind, their white garments shining in the morning air. On and on they came: men, children, women, all ages journeying together towards the Tree so that they might understand the limit of their knowledge.

Anna and the children walked immediately behind the Counsellors. Anna moved as if in a dream, but Nathan stared ahead intently, his face blanched with anticipation, and Rachel clung to her brother's hand, taking comfort from his firm clasp.

The people did not speak, but walked in concentrated silence. It was not until the Tree came into view, rising out of the earth in its magnificent strength, that they gasped in wonder and murmured aloud their awe, automatically hastening their footsteps, moving now to the tune of the River as it sang its icy song beside them.

And so they came to the Tree, host upon host, on and on, a swelling tide of white upon the plain, and the spreading arms of the Tree sheltered them all. They flung back their heads so they could see the gleaming fruit hanging above them and, through the leaves, the branches climbing up towards the infinite light beyond. Then they sent up a great shout that carried right across the plain and echoed amongst the distant mountains so that the glaciers tingled with the sound and the air mouthed the message above the peaks and sent it back to them upon its frosty tongue.

"GALEN! GALEN!"

How long they waited they did not know. No leaf stirred and no form moved as the Tree bowed over the watching people. They gazed across the plain to the far foothills, straining their eyes in anticipation, but no tall, graceful figure appeared in the distance, white hair tumbling towards his shoulders, and no answering cry rang across the land to chase away the echoes with its powerful voice.

"GALEN! GALEN!"

Only Nathan and the Counsellors noticed that Anna did

not call aloud her husband's name with the people, but gazed silently at the Tree as if she saw something there that perturbed her.

"What is it, Mother?" whispered Nathan as their companions stood with closed eyes, concentrating upon listening for a response from their lost friend.

"There is a gap amongst the branches where an apple should be, and I am afraid, for I can taste its flesh on my tongue and it is sour and bitter and will not go away. That is why I cannot call the name of Galen."

"No," urged Nathan, "you are imagining something that need never be. I can see no space amongst the branches. Close your eyes and call my father back to you."

Anna ran her tongue over her dry lips and slowly shook her head.

"It is impossible."

"No, you must not say such things, for if you do not call him, how will he ever return to us?"

His mother did not reply but gazed upwards with glittering eyes and swayed back and forwards slightly as if in pain.

Nathan felt a firm hand upon his shoulder; it was Hedron.

"We believe we have felt his presence and, as yet, we think the threads between us are unbroken. There is hope."

But Anna had moved away from the shelter of the Tree and stood alone beneath the burning sun. Between her teeth she tasted the fruit and, however forcefully she brought the saliva to her mouth, she could not drown its flavour.

Galen's grandmother had not journeyed with her people to the Tree. For three days and nights she had remained in her chair by the window, never closing her eyes or lapsing for one moment from her vigil. She sensed the cry of the people and mouthed his name also, but no hope rose to release her from her watching fear.

"Come home, Galen." She held out her arms to the laughing boy, the smiling man. "I draw you with all the love of our people, of the countless ages of our daily rhythm. Come back home. "

She waited and thought for a moment that she felt the threads around her heart stir faintly as grasses might move beneath a gentle breeze. She listened, and heard the footsteps coming towards her through the empty house. Without turning her head she knew that Anna stood beside her.

"I have been at the Tree, Grandmother, and the Counsellors sense that the threads leading to Galen are not yet broken and that he will return to us, safe and whole."

The old lady looked at the young woman. How beautiful she appeared standing beside the window in the midday light, her fair hair shining in the sunshine, her white robe falling in graceful folds.

"You should not have let him go, Anna."

"I had no choice, he was determined. I thought that if I let him go he would return."

"He was seeking knowledge that drew him away from the love of our people. Your love for him has accompanied him on that search and, in some way, made him thirst for revelation. If ever he tries to assuage that thirst, then he is, we are..." She faltered as Anna stepped closer, eyes glittering, a crimson flush upon her white cheeks.

"You protected him and kept the secret of that first journey from the Counsellors."

"I made a profound and terrible mistake," whispered the old woman, "and ever since that time I have struggled to heal the wounds inflicted upon Galen."

"Do not speak so, you do not know what you are saying! Galen is all love and goodness, he is not wounded in any way. The Counsellors have said that he will return."

"The Counsellors are the wisest of our people, but even they cannot foresee everything. How could they, for they obey the law of the mighty Tree? They sense the forbidden knowledge, but never reach to grasp it in their hands."

"What are you saying, Grandmother? You do not know what you are saying!"

"What I say comes from years of watching and praying, of trying to be a pure vessel of love. But that vessel was cracked thirty years ago, Anna, and with it was damaged the most precious thing in my life. What happened to me could have been repaired perhaps, but to Galen…"

In the distance they could hear the voices of the family approaching, returning from their journey to the Tree. There was little time. Anna spoke quietly.

"You are tired and need rest; close your eyes and sleep now. Have faith in Galen as I do."

"There will be no sleep for me until Galen returns. We should not need to have faith in each other in that way; there should only be one source of faith in our lives and that is…"

"Shush, sleep now," intoned Anna and, puckering her mouth in readiness, she glided towards the old lady. "There, you will sleep now," she whispered, and slid from the room as silently as any shadow.

# Chapter 22

Galen gazed in amazement. He had dreamt of this moment so often that now it had come he could only stand staring, hypnotised with awe. The wall towered over him, its dark and sombre surface blocking out the burning heat of the sun, a vast barrier of stone cutting the land in two, impassive in its brooding blankness.

How long he stood there he did not know. Time sank into the stones whilst day grew ever darker, drawing the cold within its embrace so that Galen began to shiver violently. He thought of his cloak, lost in the woods, and longed for its protective warmth.

"I cannot see," he whispered. It was then he thought he heard a voice calling from the other side of the wall. Words of response beat in his brain but he was unable to reply for his tongue seemed frozen in his mouth. Panic-stricken, he struggled to move his head, to tear his tongue from the roof of his mouth. In the depth of those blind moments he thought he heard the sound again and, at the same time, the sky grew lighter and he could move once more.

The wall looked vaster than ever. His hands throbbed and burnt, but it was the pain around his heart that made him groan, for it felt as though a freezing river surged across his chest, numbing the threads that linked him to his people.

"Wait for me," he implored, as fleetingly he saw before his eyes the Centre of Worship and the numberless congregation. But he could not open his lips to sing and, even as he searched for the words that would join him to his people, his hands were stretching out towards the wall. "Boy! Boy! Are you there?" he cried, shouting louder and louder, throwing back his fair head so that the sound might scale the rocky barrier and find the listener. There was no reply, and he dare not press his ear against the wall's surface as he had done as a child in case there was no answering call, but the echoed noises of thirty years ago.

He knew what he must do, and he did not pause to look behind or take counsel with himself, but began to climb. The feat seemed impossible but somehow he found the handholds and footholds he needed as, little by little, he hauled himself up towards the summit. In his desperate concentration he dare not look down the way he had come, so he did not see the thin body lying upon the ground observing him through eyes that never flickered, though the head swayed monotonously from side to side. Nor did he allow his eyes to picture the apple lying motionless where he had thrown it, or see the rotting flesh in the place where his teeth had bitten the ruby skin.

The sun burst on him as he climbed and seemed to penetrate his body until sweat drenched his head. He groaned aloud with the physical effort, wincing as the torn skin of his hands caught on the rough surface. Yet nothing mattered but the struggle to gain height and nothing else existed but the desire to reach the summit. Even as his arms grew weaker and he began to think he could not hold on much longer, his fingers closed over a flat surface and, with a last tremendous effort, he pulled himself to the top and lay there shedding tears of joy and relief.

It was some time before he felt strong enough to sit up and look about him, but when he did the sight made him gasp and rise to his knees. He had climbed further than he thought, so that the wall fell dizzily away beneath him and the ground appeared shrunken. Whether he looked in front or turned his head to gaze behind, the wall drew its implacable line forever onwards across the land, and he knelt alone upon its summit and saw emptiness on either side. The wind was rising, lifting his blond hair, and the sun burned stronger than ever. He was quite alone.

"Where are you? Where are you?"

At first he thought that the dark spot moving up the other side of the wall towards him was a shadow. He watched it for some time, puzzled and apprehensive, until a sudden glimpse of a pale face shrouded by black curls penetrated his consciousness. Then he knew he had found him at last and his search was over. Trembling, he waited until the hand came close enough for him to grasp, then he seized it in his own and, a moment later, the two men knelt together on the summit.

White darkness, black against shimmering fair, the blue-green ice fires plunging deep in liquid pools, the children, holding in each other's arms the bodies of men. Their tears flowed unchecked, and through the falling water they saw clearly the image of their quest.

"I had to find you," said Galen, "for I felt you lost in a world beyond my knowledge. I heard your cries for help and wished to save you."

"I had to find you." Lukas struggled for the right words. "I heard sounds from your side of the wall that made me think you would help me find peace."

They were kneeling back now, gazing at each other. Galen could not stop the words which came from his lips.

"I had to know; the desire to help comes from the longing to know."

It seemed an eternity until Lukas spoke again.

"I have a surfeit of knowledge, but little understanding. I want to shed my knowledge and be a child again."

"I am a child of the light," murmured Galen as he wept, and Lukas choked upon his own tears as he felt the other man's sadness and the bond between them.

"Your hands are bleeding." He looked with concern at the blood seeping from the jagged skin.

"It is nothing, I hurt myself falling from the wall thirty years ago. It is only recently that I noticed it again. It will mend now." Briefly he touched the hand of the other man and looked at him enquiringly.

"It will heal," said Lukas, "now we've found each other."

They were silent for a while as the wind blew their hair about their heads and the sun shone upon their white faces. At last Galen spoke.

"What is your world? I must know."

"Don't ask, Galen Nodeef; even to approach the question is dangerous. Your goodness must not be touched by the knowledge of where I come from. Take me home with you."

"I see across to your land, Lukas, and in the far distance, I can make out great buildings from which comes a roaring noise; but I can also glimpse the flowing ground and the trees that bend above it."

"Don't look, there is nothing there for you to see."

"How do you know my name?"

They smiled together and Lukas turned to gaze over the side of the wall Galen had climbed. He gasped at the shimmering light spread before him and the beckoning loveliness of the land below. A great warmth enveloped him.

"Oh, Galen, your land is so beautiful, like nothing I've ever seen!"

Galen did not reply, for when he looked in the direction of Lukas's pointed finger he saw only the barren ground where he had flung the apple.

They knelt before each other and felt the gulf of the unshared years between them, and they held out their arms to each other and gripped each other's hands. Far from softening as they talked, the yearning in both their hearts seemed to have increased, and they looked into each other's eyes in bewilderment.

"I'd always thought that, if we ever met, we'd know what to do," said Lukas.

"I thought the same," murmured Galen as his eyes moved from Lukas's face to gaze across his shoulders at the land he sought to discover.

The wind was lessening and the sun stumbled as the mist stole upon it, blotting out the vista all around them so that the two men were wrapped in swirling vapour.

"As soon as this clears we will climb down my side of the wall and I will take you to my people." Galen's muffled voice came from a mouth that was damp with beaded moisture, and Lukas could only press Galen's hands in thankfulness, for his own throat was dry with emotion. The mist evaporated almost as soon as it had come and they looked about eagerly, although the sun now hurt their eyes. Lukas's face was alive with excitement.

"When we're on the ground on your side of the wall everything will become clear."

Galen nodded.

"Come, let's us be on our way. The day is lengthening and we must find shelter before nightfall."

They rose to their feet and stood together but, even as they prepared to go down, Galen hesitated. He shielded his eyes with his hand and stared first one way and then another, turning again to gaze across the side from which he felt sure he had come.

"What's the matter, Galen?" Lukas was watching him with concern.

"It is strange but the views seem to have changed, for the ground looks the same on both sides of the wall. I am not sure which side we must descend to my own land."

186

"That can't be! The two sides are quite different," and Lukas too held his hand before his eyes and stared intently, first one way, then the other.

Galen spoke the truth: both ways looked the same. Whichever direction they gazed, the ground below stretched away rocky and bare. There was no shimmering light, no flowing swathes of green, only unending aridity all around them.

"I don't understand," Lukas whispered, "we must remember which way we came."

Together they dropped back their heads and held wide their arms, looking upwards as if for a sign from the tinder sky, then they fell once more to their knees and stared around them.

"Look!" Galen's voice was hoarse. "Look, on this side of the wall it is sheer and smooth; it would be impossible to climb down it. But see, on the other side there are marked places where we can rest our feet and hold tightly with our hands. This is obviously the way we must descend."

"Why, yes, yes!" Excitedly Lukas leant over, first one side, then the other. Galen was right, for one way the climb down looked comparatively easy whilst the other appeared impossible. "However did I come up that way?"

Galen shook his head.

"I understand no more than you, but this side must lead to my land and my people. Come, let's begin." Yet still he paused for a moment and held his hand to his heart. Lukas saw him frown and shake his head slightly.

"Are you alright, Galen?"

"It is nothing. I am worrying unnecessarily – searching for something that must be there if I knew how to reach it. Now is not the time."

"You are looking for a sign from your people, aren't you?" Lukas's voice was soft. "I felt your love for them even as you contemplated coming with me to the other side of the wall."

Galen's mouth broke into a smile that lit the ivory face with warmth.

"Come then, let us go. You sense what I cannot feel at the moment, but together we will find the way back to my people."

Galen led the way. As he lowered himself over the side of the wall Lukas held his wrists firmly and, when he had found the first secure footholds, he halted and looked into the eyes of his companion. Blue and green locked together, they saw clearly the hope and trepidation that united them. After a few moments Lukas released his grasp of Galen's arms and carefully slid over the side too, grateful for the other man's guiding hand on his foot, relieved when he had wedged himself firmly against the stone. They descended slowly, breathlessly, encouraging each other, helping each other, until at last they stood safely on the ground and the wall towered over them, huge in its crushing density.

They both waited for a sign that would show them where they were. It was Lukas who saw the water first and he trembled with dismay.

"Is there a large lake on your side of the wall, Galen, a lake at the foot of the mountains?"

"I can see streams and mountains in the distance." Galen looked puzzled and confused. "But there is no lake such as you describe."

Lukas gazed around with dawning horror.

"We've come down the wrong side of the wall! We're in my land, not yours. Quickly, Galen, we must climb up again and go down the other side. How could we have made such a mistake?"

He took a step towards the base, but Galen was shaking his head and pointing upwards.

"Look, I can no longer make out the footholds and handholds. We dare not attempt the ascent, the danger is too great."

Lukas ran to the wall and jumped up against it, scrambling frantically to find a jutting piece of stone, to show Galen that he was mistaken. He fell heavily to the ground and there, before his face, he imagined he saw the mutilated body, whilst close by lay the stick with which he had beaten it. He leapt to his feet in terror, suppressing the garbled words that rose from his throat. Galen had not seen, for now he was gazing ahead and a small smile hovered around his lips and his tongue slipped from his mouth and moistened them gently.

"Lukas, Lukas, your land is full of flowers and water. Why, it has a great beauty. Come, take me to your people. When the time is right we will return together to my home and share the special nature of my world."

Lukas stared up at the wall and then turned to look at the path that led towards the distant lake, the path he had walked along such a short time before.

"You promise me, Galen, that we will find our way back here and cross over to your people?"

"Of course I promise, Lukas. Now we have found each other at last we will never again be parted and, if I do not return to my land and my people before too long, I will not survive."

Lukas looked comforted and Galen smiled.

"Have faith. The wall has been breached and the great chasm between us closed. Whichever way we go we have no choice now but to travel the same path."

Lukas nodded, forgetting for the moment his earlier fears of the consequences if they could not find their way back to Galen's land.

Along the rock-strewn path they went, towards the lake

that sparkled in the distance. Lukas led the way and, when they reached the water's edge, he gazed for a long time at the rippling surface. He saw the rough mound of earth by the water where the flowers, laid so carefully, were withered and dying, and he felt the weight of the water on his chest. Galen looked troubled.

"Why do your tears come now?"

"He doesn't know," thought Lukas, "he doesn't realise what it is." The idea was disturbing in some way, made Galen seem a stranger and, for a brief moment, Lukas hesitated. Was he taking a terrible risk introducing Galen into his world? He would talk to him when they rested for the night.

"The lake is so beautiful; the sight of it moved me to tears," he said and Galen made no reply.

They went on in silence walking steadily and, as time passed, Lukas became more and more puzzled. At first he did not recognise where they were but, after a while, he started to see familiar landmarks and realised that they were drawing closer to the town. He stopped and looked around in astonishment.

"I don't understand, it took days to find the lake when I was searching for you, even though when I was a boy I'd stumbled on it so easily. It was the journey that made my..." Lukas hesitated. "My mind must be playing some trick, we can't have reached here so quickly."

"This is good for it means that when the time comes for us to return to my people, the way will not be difficult, and now we do not have to find shelter for the night."

"Yes, it must be good."

Lukas walked in a daze, his head beating painfully, worried that he had not spoken to Galen about his fears and doubts. It was too late now. Galen stayed close by his side as they drew closer and closer to the outskirts, looking about in increasing amazement, and once or twice he opened his mouth as if to ask a question, but he did not speak.

And so it was that, as the sun flared and started its final descent to the horizon, they came to the town and passed side by side between the shadowed confines of its first buildings.

## Chapter 23

It was sunset and Claire stood outside the house gazing down the road. She had watched each day at this time since Lukas's departure. Now she rubbed her eyes and stared again. In the distance two tall figures walked towards her and she felt his presence even as she struggled to identify him. She began to run, forgetting her previous anger, her determination to reject him if he came back. Only as he drew nearer did she see the dark curls tumbling around his head and realise that the man walking at his side had hair the colour of sun-drenched snow, and was a complete stranger to her. Something prevented her from running into her husband's arms and she stopped before the men, gasping for breath, unable to find the words of greeting. It was Lukas who spoke, taking the other man by the arm and leading him to Claire.

"This is a very old friend of mine, Galen Nodeef. I've asked him to come and stay with us for a while."

The blue eyes drenched Clare with their intensity and she could only nod her acquiescence, the rising questions falling away even as they flooded into her mind. The two men were waiting, and across her shoulders she felt the burden of their expectations.

"He's very welcome." She saw her husband's face relax. "You're most welcome," she repeated as Galen looked down into her eyes again before pressing his cheek to hers and placing his lips upon her forehead.

Galen moved into the house like a white shadow. After his first spontaneous reaction to Claire he had withdrawn into himself, seldom speaking, his eyes constantly restless. He absorbed the interior of the house without comment and each passing moment he looked a little more strained, his skin a little more translucent. For the first few days he never left the house and, after Lukas departed for work, Claire often found their visitor standing by a window staring bleakly into the distance.

The children were fascinated by the stranger and, at the same time, afraid of him. Behind his back they laughed at his manner of dressing, their amusement intensified when he refused the loan of any of their father's everyday clothes but went about the house swathed in an old white towelling robe for a day whilst Claire washed his own travel-stained garments. Yet there was something about him that made them falter even as they thought they could mock. They felt they should know him and yet he was completely unknown. They felt that in some way he loved them and yet held them as unfit. In their growing bewilderment they tried to avoid him.

Claire was in a state of constant tension. The momentary sense of relief and peace she felt when Galen kissed her had vanished, and now she struggled for control, both of the situation and herself. She watched her husband constantly, trying to puzzle out what was different about him. Before he had gone away there had been a great distance between them, but in some way a kind of balance in their relationship had remained. Now she felt isolated because he no longer seemed concerned about any intimacy with her, not even the destructive intimacy of the past. He appeared both more alive and yet withdrawn; his eyes glowed their green fire, yet his touch made her feel cold. He was loving to her and the children, but she felt she had lost him. He had only been gone a few days, yet it seemed an eternity since the day he had departed.

She tried to draw him towards her by telling him the news

of his grandmother.

"She's completely disappeared, Lukas, there's no trace of her. There's been such a hue and cry, police and everything. They're still looking for her, but they think she's just wandered off. I wish you'd been here; now you're back you'll have to see the police."

Lukas had his back to her and did not reply at first.

"Old people can do unexpected things sometimes. She never liked that home."

Claire was astonished.

"Lukas, I'm talking about your grandmother, do you understand? Please look at me." His silent back infuriated her and she lashed out at him. "She went missing at the same time that you left."

Now he turned and she stepped back in fear from the white mask of his face and the eyes that burned even as they froze her heart.

"You don't know what you're saying. I tell you, my grandmother will be safe and I'll know when it's right to search for her."

Claire was struggling against her tears, searching for a reply, when a noise at the doorway attracted their attention. Galen stood there, and before his stricken look Claire could only catch her breath and try to suppress her sobs. He had heard every word they said.

"I didn't mean anything. Lukas, Galen, don't look at me like that."

She ran from the room whilst the men remained motionless for a moment.

"What do I do, Galen?" Lukas whispered.

"I too have left behind a grandmother who has blessed me with her love since I was a child. I think of her constantly as I know she does of me. Your grandmother will be doing the same."

"Oh, Galen, you don't understand. It's not the same. I feel I have killed my grandmother!"

"Killed her?" Galen shook his head, unable to understand what Lukas was saying.

"Took away her life, I feel as if I took away her life."

"No! No, such an idea is unthinkable, impossible. Life is given back to its source and we who are left behind allow it to go. I do not know what you are saying."

They stared at each other in distress, longing to help each other, at a loss to know how.

"I thought that, if we could only find one another again, I would discover the answer, but I see nothing but incomprehensible reflections and pain. What have we done, Lukas? Your love and friendship is as I had imagined all those years, but everything else…" He looked about the room, out of the window, his eyes filled with fear.

"We came down the wrong side of the wall." Lukas's voice was hoarse. "It was a mistake but, at the right time, we will find our way back to your land. Have patience, Galen, there must be a reason why you're here."

"Forgive me but I have to be alone for a while."

He was gone. Lukas heard his footsteps on the stairs and knew that he would be standing at his bedroom window, gazing across the unfamiliar ground, longing for his people.

On the fourth morning after Lukas's return Claire stood in the kitchen sorting out the debris from breakfast. The children were at school and, very reluctantly, Lukas had gone to work. She had turned on the radio to distract herself as she meandered through her tasks and so did not hear Galen enter the room. She jumped with fright when he spoke.

"I am going out, Claire, I do not know when I will be back."

A weak sun shone through the window onto her dark hair as she gazed at him.

"Who are you and where do you come from?"

He stepped away from her and shook his head.

"If I am not here when Lukas returns, tell him I am searching; he will understand."

Still she delayed him, eager to break his reserve a little, to have some idea of whom and what this stranger was.

"Galen, you have not left the house until now, how will you know where to go? And you're not dressed…" She faltered, feeling suddenly ashamed, looking at his white garments, feeling the blood rise to her cheeks. "I mean, I could lend you…"

"Please, Claire, I must go."

"Wait, you cannot leave without taking some refreshment with you."

"I need nothing, please let me go."

"No wait! Do!" In her insistence she became almost girlish. She ran to the sideboard and took something from the back. He had not noticed before; how had he not noticed? She was walking towards him, her arm stretched out before her, and on the palm of her hand lay the offering. "Take it," she said smiling, "and eat it when you're hungry."

The sweat glistened upon his forehead.

"Where did you get this from?"

"Where? What a funny question. See here."

Then he saw the bowl of fruit upon the side board and tasted again, between his teeth, the flesh that rotted even as you took the first bite. With a roar of pain he smashed the apple from Claire's hand and rushed from the room, leaving her standing frightened and amazed, the bruised apple lying at her feet.

When Lukas returned that evening Claire did not tell him

about the events of the morning, except that Galen had left the house quite early taking nothing with him and, as yet, he had not returned.

"But where was he going?" asked Lukas again and again until she could bear it no more.

"He said he was going to search, he said you would understand. Lukas, what is going on? I'm frightened."

"Nothing is going on." Lukas was shouting and his face was whiter than ever. "That's the whole trouble." Claire looked at him in horror as into her head sprung the memory of Galen's face as he knocked the apple from her hand.

"I think you're going mad, I think you're both mad."

"Don't say that, you mustn't say that!"

He ran from the room and, a moment later, she heard him opening the front door. At first she thought he must have left her again, but then through the window she saw him standing outside gazing along the way Galen should return.

The children were in bed, and night had long since fallen, when finally they heard the quiet knock at the front door. Galen stood outside, his whole body sagging with an appalling weariness, his blue eyes sunk into the back of his head, his white hair framing the dull ivory of his face. He stumbled into Lukas's arms and clung to him, moaning incoherently.

"Quickly, Claire, fetch some water!" She ran at his bidding, although they had not spoken to each other for hours. Lukas cradled Galen as if he were a tiny child and, when the water came, he held the cup gently against the pale lips.

"Galen, speak to me." Slowly Galen's breathing steadied and his eyes focused upon Lukas's anguished face.

"I cannot say what I have seen. I have been walking all day and now I understand the sounds I heard as I lay with my ear against the wall when I was a child. Oh, why did I not listen to the Counsellors?"

Lukas wept in sympathy and tried to offer comfort.

"Galen, let's leave at once and return to the wall. Somehow we will climb it and go to your people. I can't be certain what you heard that day, or what you've seen today, but I can begin to guess. I do know, though, how I felt as I lay against the wall when I was a boy, listening to those sounds. That's why I've longed ever since to find you. In all my dreams of meeting you again I never imagined that you would come home with me. Why should anyone want to come here? We made a mistake together and climbed down the wrong side of the wall, but surely we can put that right. We must go to your people, whoever, wherever they are. Let's go at once."

But Galen did not seem to hear and, all the time Lukas was speaking, he stared at Claire as if hypnotised.

"I knew when you tried to give me the apple. I would not take it, but already it was too late for me to refuse."

"What are you talking about?" groaned Lukas. "I don't understand."

"You're mad!" cried Claire, gazing in horror at the two men. "You're both mad! What's happening? Stop looking at me like that; I've nothing at all to do with this. Galen, you can't stay here any longer. Lukas, tell Galen he must go."

Lukas did not even hear her.

"It's never too late, Galen, never. We can atone for our mistakes."

"Atone?"

"Work for forgiveness, make up for the wrong we've done, the mistakes we've made, start again."

"Wrong, mistakes; I have never heard of such things. I am lacking in strength, Lukas, and I cannot begin a journey yet although I long to. I am unable to find any rhythm here and its lost notes beat beyond my hearing and fill me with grief.

There is no peace."

"I know a place where you can find peace, Galen, don't despair. I'll take you there tomorrow and after that I'm sure you'll have the strength to begin your journey home."

"Where is that?"

Galen sounded so defeated Lukas longed to give him hope.

"It's where I go on a Sunday."

"Where you go?"

"The place I go to worship."

"Ah! Then of course I will come with you."

"What has he seen?" Claire asked Lukas later that night as they lay in bed.

"He has seen everything you and I have seen, and I can never forgive myself."

"What do you mean?" Clare was looking at him in bewilderment. "You talk in riddles. We've seen nothing so very awful, except on television."

"We are immune to much of what we see, though even for us the sights are sometimes unendurable. For Galen, the shock is enough to drive him insane."

"Who is he, where does he come from, why does he insist on wearing those strange clothes? He makes me shiver the way he looks almost straight through me, that lost, yearning expression on his face. Why doesn't he just go home and leave us alone?"

"If it were that simple he would have left by now. I don't know where he comes from, Claire."

"Then how can you say he's an old friend?"

"Because I met him once, long ago. Don't ask me any more questions now, please. Oh, what have I done?"

She looked at his pale face and sunken eyes, the hollow grief that left her feeling isolated and helpless.

"I'll take him with me tomorrow, and then I hope he'll be strong enough to go home."

"And you?"

He did not answer.

In the hush of Sunday morning, Lukas and Galen were walking along the empty road. The sky was scudded with clouds and rain threatened in the air. To Lukas's relief, Galen seemed a little better. His step was firm and he held his head tilted slightly backwards, as if he were drinking in the very essence of the day. Lukas felt his spirits lifting as he strode along beside him through the deserted streets. As they rounded a corner the spire came into view and Lukas smiled with pleasure.

"See, Galen," he said, taking the other man's arm in his eagerness to share the sight.

Galen gazed in surprise.

"Why, it is so small."

"No, no, it's quite large."

Galen did not reply but, as they came nearer to the building, he looked around keenly, although he still said nothing. Lukas was puzzled by his behaviour.

"Are you looking for someone, Galen?"

Galen shook his head.

"It is not one person I am looking for, but perhaps I am looking in the wrong places. After yesterday perhaps I should know not to look at all."

It was very quiet inside and the interior struck a little chilly and dark. A few people were gathered at the front. It was very peaceful, though, and Lukas sighed with contentment and relief. Walking forwards, it was a moment before he realised that Galen was not following him. He turned to look back, ready to beckon him with an encouraging smile, and saw that his companion was standing completely still, as if in a trance. He returned hastily to his side.

"This way." He gestured to the seated people, but Galen shook his head. Slowly, very slowly, he began to move. Lukas felt frightened and dismayed. "Galen, please come and sit with me so that we can wait together for the worship to begin."

Still the other man ignored him, or did not hear him. On he walked, on and on, watched by the startled people and the priest, who now appeared from the shadows and tried to speak to him.

At last Galen halted, and threw back his head so that the curls tumbled down his back and he spread his arms wide. As the watching people rose to their feet in consternation, he let out a great shout that echoed round the building.

"Oh grief, oh grief! What wood is this?"

Aghast, the small group of worshippers watched as Lukas and the priest tried to take Galen by the arm and comfort him, but there was no consolation they could offer. The cries of anguish fell faster and faster from his lips, until Lukas could bear it longer and flung his arms around the tortured man.

"Stop and listen to us. You've got it all wrong, you don't understand."

For a moment Galen was silent but, as Lukas and the priest tried to help him, they saw his lips moving, trying to form words as if garnered from some great depths of his soul:

"I do, I do understand, and I can never be rid of that understanding."

They tried to hold him but no strength could contain him. Hands before his face, Galen ran down the aisle and out into the hushed morning, and it seemed an eternity until his cries faded into the distance.

# Chapter 24

Lukas was growing frantic with worry about Galen. He had barely spoken for days, indeed it felt as though he hardly existed with them at all. He walked about the house in a body that seemed to be searching for its soul and his numb eyes looked blankly in front and offered no reflection. He had eaten little since his arrival, always toying with the food upon his plate, smiling apologetically as he left it almost untouched, but now he merely sipped a few drops of water and ate a morsel of bread when Lukas pressed him. He was becoming weaker and Lukas chastised himself bitterly for bringing him home. This was what his longing and searching had led to: the death of his grandmother and the agony of his friend. At night he dreamt of Galen's country and the sweet sounds he had heard from the far side of the wall but, when he awoke in the morning, his fists were clenched in the pain of the realisation that he had come so near to reaching it at last and had failed. Lukas determined that somehow he must persuade Galen to begin the journey back to the wall before it was too late.

The police had been round once to ask him about his grandmother, but they had seemed to accept his bafflement about her disappearance. Claire had not mentioned the old lady again and Lukas was relieved that the subject seemed to be forgotten in the impact of Galen's arrival. He would never be able to tell her what had happened.

"I will find the strength for both of us to make that journey," he whispered to his own strained reflection in the mirror, "I must help Galen back to his own land before he dies of grief."

Claire floated into the glass behind him, her hair drifting.

"Why do you both have the same scars on your hands?" He shook his head. "Don't go, I can't bear to lose you again."

"If I don't take Galen soon, we're lost for ever," he said as her image faded and he was alone again.

For a day or two after the incident at the church the family went through the routine of living as if nothing had happened. Lukas left early in the morning for work, returning anxiously in the evening, dreading what he might discover, fearful, hopeful, longing only to find Galen restored to his former self. Claire took the children to school and fetched them in the afternoon and, in between, she stayed at home, filling her time with tasks that didn't need doing, and watching Galen. He walked in the garden hour after hour with footsteps softer than the breeze that stirred in the hedgerows and he never spoke to her, nor came within reach of her, until Lukas returned.

"What is preventing you from leaving, Galen?" asked Lukas. "I know that you're longing to return to your people and that staying here can bring you nothing but pain. Let's go together, I'll come with you. We made a terrible mistake when we came down on this side of the wall but, once we've crossed over, your strength will return."

They were walking side by side under the dark November sky and the world seemed deserted and forlorn. There was a distinct chill in the air and Lukas thought he felt the first drops of rain.

"Something is holding me here, Lukas; it is not just that I feel my strength ebbing away. I am weaker, but that is not what is preventing me from leaving. There's something else I am compelled to know and I will not be able to go until that knowledge has been given to me. I no longer choose it, but I cannot escape it. There is a revelation that beckons me but, as yet, I do not understand its source."

"Oh, Galen, the longer we stay, the more difficult it'll be for us to retrace our steps."

"Give me just a little more time, I beg you. I have promised we will go together; when I know what awaits me I will be released, and can return with you to my own land."

It was on the tip of Lukas's tongue to ask Galen about his anguish, to suggest that nothing here could bring any release, but he remained silent. He felt the other man's pain so heavily on his heart that he thought his own would break under the burden.

The weather had changed. It was a surprisingly warm morning for November, and the children had a day off school. Claire was putting things for the day into the boot of the car: the picnic basket, rug, the paraphernalia for an outing with children. Stephen and Susie danced excitedly around her and she tried to share their pleasure, relax the tight unhappiness in her face. She had hoped Lukas would go with them for, quite unexpectedly, he had taken the day off work, but he shook his head as if her request was trivial and irrelevant. She had promised the children, though, and she could not disappoint them.

"Right, you two, into the car." It was then she saw them walking across the lawn towards her, identical in height, their heads held high, looking as graceful as the trees that swayed and whispered overhead.

"Would you mind if we came with you after all, Claire?" It was Galen who spoke and, behind the gentle question, she felt the urgency of his request. Lukas shrugged his shoulders and smiled and she did not ask him why he had changed his mind and, above all, why Galen wished to accompany them.

"Of course, you know we'd love to have you with us. I

204

hope you won't mind the squash in the car – I think you had better sit in the front."

Galen looked at the car as if it were some unknown animal.

"For me everything is new, yet somehow strangely old." As he climbed inside he glanced up at the sky to where the sun shone over them with its golden smile.

They had eaten their picnic lunch sitting on a rug on the grass and now the children ran around whilst the adults rested quietly. It was growing chilly and soon they would have to move. Once again Galen had only taken a little bread and water, but he was looking stronger and Lukas felt more hopeful about him.

"How good you are, Lukas," said Galen, turning to the dark-haired man, "trying to imbibe me with your strength. I am feeling much better. I sense that my time here is ending and soon I will be able to begin the journey home."

"We," prompted Lukas, and the other man nodded. Claire looked at the two men and said nothing.

Galen had heard vague sounds of animals in the distance all morning, but they meant nothing to him. Whilst the others explored he had remained behind, pleased to be alone. He had no idea what the others were doing, and had been deaf to the children's excited chatter as they left him. Every now and then he had put his hand to his heart, and each time he frowned as he took it away. His hands throbbed painfully today, but around his heart there was no tugging sensation to bring him comfort.

"I am not yet myself," he had thought, "I must have patience."

He had been aware all morning of one particular building some distance away, but he had not moved from his position or given it more than an occasional glance. Yet he knew he would go to it, however much he pretended it was not there.

Now he could wait no longer.

"I am going for a small walk."

Claire nodded, but Lukas jumped to his feet.

"I'll come with you."

"I am best alone, thank you, I will soon return."

Galen smiled and Lukas felt he had no choice but to let him go, though some unprompted fear made him long to take his friend by the arm and lead him far away.

Galen walked slowly. Although he knew that he must reach his destination, the closer he drew the more he wondered why he had left the companionship of Lukas to cross to this unknown territory. The words upon the wall of the squat red building made no sense to him. He read them several times shaking his head. Yet he was sure that he had found the right place and that he must enter.

Astonishment was his first sensation. How could a tree, even a small one, grow inside a building? In places its branches touched the roof and there was a small seat around the trunk, although there was little shelter to be found beneath the boughs. There were quite a few people wandering around the building but Galen took no notice of them and was not aware of their inquisitive stares. He followed the dark shadow of one of the branches. It led him to the glass along the walls. He felt a sense of coldness that gripped his lungs and throat and stopped him breathing, but he was compelled to look.

He saw it moving very slowly towards him across the twigs and stones and small rocks. Dry skin, flat head, the body coiling and uncoiling as it approached, eyes small and hard, unflickering, staring into his as it sought to lock his gaze, swaying the triangle of its head so that he must follow its motion with his own eyes, eyes which flickered involuntarily beneath the fixed, dead stare. The body, obscenely beautiful, rippled along the other side of the glass and the expressionless face never ceased its rhythmical concentration, and its tongue tasted his terror.

"No, no!" He beat his fists upon the pane. "No, no!" He wept and raged until his face became distorted and his eyes started in horror from a skull that crackled the bone and blood of despair.

A crowd was gathering around him, gazing in astonishment.

"What's wrong with him?"

"Someone needs to do something."

"Can I help you?"

The words spun around him in meaningless gibberish and he backed away from the glass holding his hands over his eyes, calling aloud.

"Jedra, Jedra, what have I done?"

Blindly he ran from the building still clasping his hands in front of his face, brushing aside the hands that reached out to stop him.

Lukas and Claire saw him fleeing towards them and his tormented cries reached their ears long before they could hear what he was saying. Lukas jumped to his feet and sped towards the racing figure. He held out his arms to him, struggling to understand what he said.

"I must leave at once, I have misunderstood everything. I always thought I knew better than the rest of my people, even the Counsellors. Oh! What have I done?"

"Galen, what has happened?" Lukas was close to panic. He could not understand what had changed. All he knew was that Galen was distraught and he could not help him.

Claire and the children stood watching, their faces frightened and bewildered. Susie was crying and Stephen clung to his mother's hand.

"Lukas," Claire whispered, "what's the meaning of this? Who *is* Galen?"

For a moment Lukas looked at his wife, then he turned to

the trembling man beside him.

"I thought when I found you all my questions would fall away and there'd be only answers that brought peace. Now I see that my mistake has created nothing but a world that gives no answers that can ever satisfy."

"I sought knowledge," whispered Galen, "and my appetite so numbed me that I could no longer taste the food of my people. I sought knowledge and, because I would not rest beside the wood of the Tree, I was taken to the wood upon the table, and the fruit of the Tree led to the bruised flesh upon the ground, and the taking of the fruit for my solitary journey led to the meeting with the creature that Jedra saw, the creature that now writhes upon its stomach. Oh what have I done? My search for you, Lukas, has brought only torment to us both. Let me go back to my people and my land."

"I've never stopped you, Galen," groaned Lukas.

"I do not know what I am saying. I must leave at once. The threads have gone from around my heart and I am desperate to reach the wall so that I can feel them again."

"I'm coming with you! We'll find the way together."

"Please, Lukas, remain here; I fear that if you come with me I will never be able to reach my people."

"If I don't come, Galen, I fear you'll never find your way back to the wall. There's no choice but for us to go together; it was always going to be this way."

Galen nodded.

"Perhaps you are right."

Over the fence they saw the road stretching away into the distance, the sun shining upon its empty surface. For a moment Lukas enfolded Claire and the children in his arms. They clung to one another, briefly united in the sorrow of parting.

"I'm sorry."

She knew it was useless to try to stop him, she had known that for a long time. When he released them she held the children close and watched him through blurred eyes. Galen and Lukas stood side by side and the blue and green fires blazed with longing and apprehension. They paused for a few seconds, then turned and began to run, slowing down briefly to climb the fence, along the road's dark surface, until their forms, diminished by distance, were impossible to tell apart.

## Chapter 25

They ran swiftly side by side, the pounding urgency of their feet beating the same rhythm upon the ground. If they passed anyone they did not notice, for they stared incessantly ahead, straining their eyes as if trying to draw the unseen horizon into view. On and on they sped, hair flying back from their white faces, unaware of the changing surfaces beneath their feet, the landscape that fell away behind them.

"Run," they gasped to each other, "run faster!" and the sun blazed down upon them and parched their mouths, even as it drew the glistening moisture onto their skins. The town shrank and shrivelled over their shoulders, whilst ahead, the hills rose in green promise and the ribbon of the road led them on towards the skyline.

On they raced, down lanes, through tunnels of trees, on over fields and streams, until at last they were leaping across hillsides, following the curve of the land downwards towards the misty distance. Only then did Lukas slacken his pace and turn excitedly to Galen.

"I can smell it!"

"What, what?" Galen did not wish to waste a moment; he wanted to run without stopping until they reached the wall.

"The water, the scent of water. We must be getting close to the lake."

Galen laughed aloud for the first time since he had left his land. Tossing back his head he took great reviving breaths.

"It is the scent of water, we have found it!"

With renewed energy they sped on until, ahead of them, they saw the lake shimmering in the sunlight and, in the far distance, the mountains keeping watch from their snow-drenched summits. On they raced down the long slope to where the ground flattened out, and at their feet lay the valley of flowers, invading their nostrils with its potent scent, unfurling its rainbow carpet.

"Come," cried Galen, "there is no time for us to linger," and they moved forward as one flesh, springing over the heads of the delicate flowers so that the crushed perfumes clung to the soles of their boots.

At the lakeside they threw themselves to their knees, splashing the cool water over their faces, cupping their hands to fill them with the refreshing liquid so that they could drink. As their breathing grew steadier they started to look around. Galen stared at the path running by the side of the lake, the one that branched away towards the mountains, the route that led to the wall, but Lukas was searching for something else. He wanted to tell Galen, but paused as he remembered the other man's bewilderment when he had pointed to the grave before, and his distress when Lukas talked of the death of his grandmother. He jumped to his feet and walked a little way up and down the lake side, but the grave was not there. He tried to suppress a rising panic; it must be somewhere, his memory was faulty and he was looking in the wrong place. He shivered. Galen watched him for a while, and his face was troubled.

"We must go quickly, Lukas, there is no time to stay here. Once we have crossed the wall back to my land, everything will become clear and we will be able to rest."

Reluctantly Lukas had to agree for, although Galen was quite calm now, the look of terror that had taken possession of his face earlier still lingered behind his eyes.

"I'm coming." He ran after the fair-haired man, along the path by the side of the lake, away from the place where she must lie. Every now and then he glanced back, but the ground remained flat to his view and no rising mound of earth interrupted its flow to bring him comfort. He had no choice but to keep moving, yet the memory of that day when he and his grandmother had found the lake together so many years ago swept over him. He could not bear to think of her lost somewhere and alone in that deserted place. She never would have abandoned him, but surely if she was still alive she would understand why he could not let Galen go on without him. He started to run faster. "I've seen this route before, I'll lead the way now."

On they pounded, through the grass that straggled at their ankles, feeling the pressure upon their knees as the ground became rocky and unyielding, stumbling occasionally as a stone caught at their feet. Lukas felt Galen's breath upon his neck and ran to the beating of Galen's heart as if it were his own. On and on they raced, staring intently ahead the whole time, whilst the sun beat mockingly upon their heads and burned their sore eyes. At last they could run no more and they stood together gasping and looked around. Galen held out his arms.

"Come shadow, throw yourself across our path. Then we will see the wall towering over us and we can put our ears against it and hear the music of my people; then we will be able to climb over it and so return to my land, to the River which will still be singing its song, and to the mighty Tree."

Lukas did not understand all that Galen said, but a longing swept over him so strongly that he wanted to shout aloud. He turned to the other man and tried to offer comfort.

"The wall must be near. We'll find it."

"If we don't find it, Lukas, what shall I do?"

"We will, you must believe we will!"

Galen did not reply.

They gazed into the distance straining their eyes, willing the stones to rear up before them but, however much they stared, they saw only an endless vista of bare landscape and burning sky. After a long time they turned to face each other and, in the glistening blue and green, they perceived the beauty that could create and could destroy.

They saw the shadow then, far away across the rocky ground.

"Someone is coming towards us," whispered Lukas, "do you see?"

Galen had seen. Rigid with anticipation he watched as the form came closer, step by step, over the barren ground.

"Do not stir," he breathed, "until we know what it is that approaches."

They waited whilst the moisture sprung from their brows and their hands clenched and unclenched, leaving the marks of their nails on the palms. The figure drew ever nearer until it stopped a little way from them, and stood in silence. Lukas gasped.

"Why, it's only a child!"

Fair curls, white clothing, the small, soft black boots, the ancient eyes.

"My son, my beloved son." Galen held out his arms and started to run towards the boy, anticipating the feel of the warm hands around his neck. "How did you find me? How did you reach us? How oh how did you cross the wall?" He was becoming incoherent in his ecstasy. The people had sent Nathan to find him and lead him home.

A short distance from the boy he hesitated. Nathan had not moved and the expression upon his face was not that of a child.

"Father." His voice rang across the space between them. "Father, you must not touch me. Do not come any closer. You may not join me."

"Nathan, what are you saying? Not touch you? Why, come quickly and embrace me; I cannot bear to be separated from you any longer."

An expression flitted across the child's face that made

213

Lukas tremble but Galen, in his frenzy, did not notice.

"Please, Father, listen to me. We can no longer embrace. I have come to warn you."

"Warn me? Nathan, what are you talking about?"

"I have not long, Father; please listen to what I say."

"I will not listen for it is I who must warn *you*. I have discovered something terrible, horrifying beyond all imagining. I am coming to tell our people."

"I see it upon you."

"You are a child, you do not understand. We are wasting time. I must return immediately to our people to warn them about the creature that Jedra saw. I bring Lukas who has been searching for me since long before you were born, and who will help me when I explain everything."

Lukas stepped forward eagerly; perhaps he could help to heal this appalling breach between father and son. Nathan, however, did not appear to see him and Lukas hesitated even as the words of greeting rose to his lips. The boy was relentless in his quiet insistence.

"Father, you cannot return, the threads have broken."

"No, no, that is not true! They are a little weaker, just a little, but they are not broken."

"They are broken," whispered Nathan, and Lukas felt the tears start to his eyes as he saw the boy's pain.

"I have to warn our people," cried Galen, "if I do not, they are in great danger."

"You may not warn our people. Jedra fulfilled that task at the very beginning."

"You are only a child! You are not speaking your own words and do not understand what you are saying. I can talk with you no longer although my heart breaks with love for you. I must go to the Counsellors."

"I have come from the Counsellors, you will not find them. Father, please do not try to return."

"Anna, Rachel, my grandmother, what will become of them if I stay here, lost in an unknown world?"

For the first time since he had stood before them Nathan stirred, very slightly.

"You must not see my mother. Rachel is well cared for."

"Must not see Anna? My own wife!" The boy did not reply. "My grandmother, what about my grandmother?"

It seemed a long while before Nathan spoke again.

"Your grandmother has gone on her final journey."

"No! I cannot, I will not believe you. My grandmother would never depart without waiting to bid me farewell."

Nathan looked at his father with steady compassion but his resolve was unshakeable.

"I must go and please, I beg you, do not follow me."

Lukas could bear it no longer; his own sorrow welled up in him and he emitted forth a great shout of grief.

"Wait, Nathan, you cannot leave your father like this. I will stay behind but, if you do not take him, he cannot survive. Have pity, let him return home with you."

Weeping, Galen took Lukas's hand.

"You cannot deny me my own people, my own land!"

"You will destroy him, can't you see that?"

Still Nathan did not move towards his father, nor did he seem to notice Lukas's presence, although he responded to his words.

"If you return with me, you will destroy us all." He turned to go. "Goodbye, Father."

Galen tried to move but his legs were so heavy they pinned him to the ground.

"Wait, wait, you need my help. How will you cross the wall?"

Nathan shook his head.

"There is no wall, Father. Goodbye."

"There is a wall," shouted Galen, "there is, and we have

climbed over it."

Nathan was beginning to walk away from them, his small shoulders set firm, the curls at the back of his head shining in the sunlight.

"Wait, Nathan, my beloved son, wait. I am coming with you. You must want me to come home."

The boy did not pause or turn his head.

"No, no!" The cry seemed like a legion of sounds, echo upon echo spinning all around them, a multitude of denials, a host upon host of clear voices, all saying the same words, "No, no you cannot come."

Almost frantic now, Galen held his hands over his ears. In his own bewildered fear, Lukas tried to comfort him.

"The boy does not mean it, Galen. Speak to him again, this time he will listen. A child can't tell his father what to do."

Galen pointed ahead in despair.

"I cannot speak to him. See!"

Lukas followed the line of Galen's finger: where Nathan had stepped was only barren land and not a shadow stirred across the dusty ground to suggest life. For a few seconds they were transfixed in their dismay then, brushing the tears from his eyes in defiance, Galen threw back his head.

"You are right. I will not be denied. I will follow and my people will receive me back into their hearts as if I had never been away."

Lukas gripped his arm and nodded.

"I'm coming with you, I won't let you go alone now."

Fleetingly Galen hesitated, then he put his hand upon the shoulder of his friend and tried to smile.

"Come then, we will go together."

Lukas needed no second bidding and, following the direction Nathan had taken, they began to run once more beneath the bright and burning sky.

# Chapter 26

They had been running as fast as they could for a long time, but never once had they caught even a glimpse of a small figure in front of them.

"Your son must fly like the wind itself," gasped Lukas as they raced side by side over endless earth.

"I do not understand, for Nathan could never outpace me; he must have gone another way."

Galen's face seemed tightened over his delicate bones and Lukas felt a growing anxiety.

"Then we must have lost our route!"

He looked around fearfully as he ran, but Galen shook his head.

"Stop for a moment, I am sure I recognise that forest although I do not remember it being so large." It was painful to rest. The forest lay ahead, smothering the side of the mountain with its dense foliage, green almost to blackness. "I am certain it is the forest I passed through on my journey to the wall." He shuddered, remembering the panic he had felt amongst those silent trees.

"On your journey to the wall?" Lukas sounded incredulous. "You must be mistaken, Galen. All that you've gone through since leaving home has left you confused."

Galen shook his head slowly and gazed at Lukas with fearful eyes.

"I am not confused, I know that this forest is on my side of the wall."

"But Galen, we have not yet crossed the wall!"

"No, we have not." Galen stared back the way they had come. "Yet I am not mistaken, Lukas, I feel sure I am not; why, it was after I had escaped from the forest that I..."

"Yes?"

"It does not matter." Galen shook his head again and ran his hand over his lips as if to remove something clinging to the flesh.

"But Galen, if what you say is true and the ground we stand on really is your side of the wall, then we must have…" He could not finish, but stared in bewilderment around him.

"Yes, yes, we must be on the other side."

"It's impossible! How could that be?"

"I do not know, unless somehow we have skirted around it."

"No, Galen, no, the wall stretched right across the land. There's no way we could have missed it."

"Perhaps there is a gap in the wall we did not see before and, in our great haste, we did not notice that we had passed through."

"Nathan said that…" Lukas dare not say the words.

"Nathan is a child, what he says is of no consequence. Do not talk to me about him; I wish to forget what he said."

Galen's eyes flashed with unexpected rage and Lukas stepped back a little, suddenly afraid.

"Don't look at me like that, I won't mention your son again."

"Forgive me." Galen held out his hand, "I do not know what I am saying. You must never fear me, Lukas, nor I you."

"Oh, Galen," – Lukas was quick to respond to the gesture – "we're both overwrought, I'm not afraid of you."

Galen smiled with relief.

"Lukas, I do not understand how, but somehow we have crossed the wall."

Lukas tossed back his black curls in sudden excitement.

"Then the wall is behind us and our journey will soon be over. You've escaped from my world, Galen, and are in the land of your own people."

Galen could not stop staring at the forest and he did not seem to share Lukas's excitement and certainty, although he tried to speak with confidence.

"The terror and knowledge are on the other side of the wall and I am sure we can now travel safely."

But he remembered his cloak lost in the midst of that dark interior and shuddered slightly. Lukas was looking closely at the obstacle ahead of them and did not see his friend's misgivings.

"Somehow we have to find a path through those trees."

Galen sighed. "Yes, we have no choice."

The sun was hotter than ever and the two men had not drunk for a long time. Now they became aware of their dry mouths and parched lips, but they could do nothing to quench their thirst as they had brought no liquid with them.

"It'll be such a relief to get some shelter," said Lukas, "I'm so thirsty; do you think there's a stream near here or in the forest?"

Galen shook his head slowly.

"There is no water; we will have to wait until we come out on the other side."

From the distance the trees had presented an implacable barrier but, as they drew closer, they saw a small gap between two massive trunks and, a few moments later, they had eased their way through and were out of the burning sunlight and immersed in the gloom of the forest world.

"We must keep going straight ahead," whispered Galen, "whatever happens we must not deviate to either side."

Lukas nodded mutely. He did not like the feel of the forest despite the relief of its cool shelter, and he was anxious to move as swiftly as possible. Galen too felt uneasy. In both men's heads was the memory of a soft rustling and the sound from the past tapped its faint menace in their ears and filled the silence.

Close together, Galen leading, they made their way through the trees, unable to see more than a short distance ahead, treading upon ground that was invisible. No other living thing stirred, nor did the tight-woven leaves overhead sway for even a moment and allow light to glance in. As much as they could they held their breath, so that when the exhaled sighs came the air seemed laden with their echoes. And, however much Galen looked anxiously from side to side, peering intently through the gloom, no branch offered back his lost cloak with the protection of its warm folds.

"Will this forest never end?" groaned Lukas in despair. "We're completely lost in this suffocating silence. I'd rather be burnt by the sun than go through this."

"There is a way out on the other side; if we have patience, we will find it," and, even as Galen spoke, a tiny spot of light appeared ahead. "See, see there is light! Stay close to me and we will soon be out of here."

They stumbled into the sunlight with gasps of relief. The air seemed a little cooler on this side of the woods and, although there was still no water in sight, their thirst had lessened slightly and they could look around. Galen now seemed in the grip of a feverish excitement and his eyes swam a brilliant blue, although his face was as white as ever. He stood with his back to the trees staring up at the mountainside and in his exhilaration he held out his arms, whilst tears of relief and ecstasy ran down his cheeks.

"See the way up to the glacier? Beyond that lies the route to the great plain and the mighty Tree. We are nearing the end of our journey at last."

Lukas touched Galen on the shoulder.

"What tree is that?"

Galen started with surprise.

"Of course you do not know, I was forgetting. It is difficult to understand that you do not know. Wait a little longer and then you may see for yourself what no words of mine could ever fully describe."

"I'll wait, but I can't imagine what you're talking about."

Lukas longed to ask more pressingly, but the expression on Galen's face discouraged him, and instead he looked at the path ahead and tried to imagine what lay beyond. He was waiting for more than just knowledge, but for the feeling of harmony to flood into his soul as it had done when he knelt on the other side of the wall all those years ago.

"Come," cried Galen, "we must journey on towards the glacier."

"Glacier, do we have to cross a glacier? Why, we're not equipped."

"We will manage it, but we must be sure we are over on the other side before darkness falls. I cannot remember the length of this part of the journey; I was so filled with eagerness to reach the wall I can only remember my great excitement. We must keep going."

Lukas could only nod in agreement. They walked swiftly, gaining height so rapidly that soon the forest below looked far away, and it was difficult to believe that they had felt so uneasy and trapped within it just a little while before. The air was growing cooler all the time.

"I've so often dreamt of being with you in your land, Galen, now we are here I can't quite believe it." Lukas shivered for, despite the exertion of walking uphill, the cool breeze caught at his neck and made him cold.

"I will not feel I am home until I stand above the plain and look down upon the mighty Tree and the River. Then I will know I am indeed returned."

Galen's eyes were translucent with excitement and he bounded up the rising path with great energy, urging Lukas onwards. Lukas did not ask again what Galen meant, for something was stirring in his mind that he dimly recognised. He reached out to grasp it but, at that moment, Galen spoke again and it was gone.

As the hours of evening drew nearer and the path became steeper, so the air grew ever cooler and, in the far distance, they could hear the roar of what sounded like many waterfalls. Galen could hardly contain his excitement and anticipation, and he kept on beckoning to Lukas who now followed a little way behind. When they were beginning to think that they would never reach it, they turned a corner and the glacier lay before them in all its frozen beauty. They paused for a moment in wonder, then Lukas rushed to the edge of the ice and scraped some of the snow from the surface, cramming it into his mouth.

"I'm so thirsty, I feel as if I can never drink enough."

"I feel the same way." Galen had joined him and was sucking some melting snow from his cupped hand. "But we must keep going; night falls quickly here and we have to climb higher up this side in order to cross safely."

Lukas nodded dubiously for the ice looked treacherous and he was afraid.

"We should be roped together."

Galen shook his head.

"We need no rope," he said as the memory of Hiemal swept into his mind, and the voice screaming for help as the man fell into the icy tomb. He shuddered. "But I will lead the way and you can put your hands on my shoulders. We will go very slowly."

Lukas obeyed, his face taut with fear, and they stepped onto the glacier with a single tread and started to cross.

The cold invaded their whole bodies so that they moved with rigid steps, their teeth gritted against the sudden wind, their eyes half closed against the mist that unexpectedly swirled and clung in droplets to their shivering frames.

Crevasses sprang before them, eyeless gateways to oblivion, and the surface they walked upon offered no certainty of support.

"I can't go forward," cried Lukas, "I'm too afraid!"

"Hold on, it will pass."

Lukas obeyed for he could not see the expression of terror on the other man's face, a face that was whiter than the snow itself, eyes burning holes in the taut skin.

On over the ice they went, Lukas's hands clutching Galen's shoulders, and each step was more fearful than the one before as the glacier crackled and splintered beneath them.

"Help us," whispered Lukas repeatedly, until at last Galen paused.

"We are almost there."

Neither man needed to wipe away the tears of relief for they froze upon their cheeks even as they touched the flesh. Moments later they stumbled onto firm ground and flung themselves down, gasping with exhaustion and gratitude. When they raised their heads again they saw the opening, just visible in the gloom.


The cold within the cave struck them both and they started back in dismay.

"We have no choice," said Galen, "we have to shelter for the night up here in the mountains."

How he longed for the warmth of his cloak to wrap around them. Cautiously they crept further inside. Although they said nothing, both men felt uneasy again and feared to peer too closely into the darkness.

"This cave seems familiar." Lukas's voice was hoarse.

"It cannot be, for I slept here on my journey to the wall. I was not alone then either, for one of my brothers shared the cave with me."

"What became of him? I thought you travelled the whole way alone?"

"I did." Galen spoke abruptly. "He merely shared the shelter of the cave for one night."

Lukas asked no more questions. He remembered the fear of his grandmother as she lay beside him, and her still form as she slept. He could picture her sitting on a rock whilst he made a fire. It must be co-incidence that there was a rock of the same shape and size, in the same position, in this cave. He shook his head, trying to empty his mind. He was exhausted. He tried to smile at Galen.

"Let's try and get some sleep."

Galen nodded, for there was nothing else to be done. They had neither food nor drink, no refreshment of any kind; they could only wait for the dawn. It seemed a little warmer at the back of the cave, and here they curled close together and closed their eyes.

Despite the cold and the hardness of the ground they slept, a shallow, uneasy sleep in which they were conscious of their aching bodies and restless minds, of the chill which wrapped itself around them and made them shiver. Nevertheless, a kind of oblivion overcame them and held their lids over their eyes until the first morning light trembled on the eastern horizon.

Although the cave was submerged in gloom the men sensed the approach of dawn. They scrambled out even as the light surged fully into the sky and held out the gift of morning to them in its scarlet and blue embrace. Galen's eyes glittered with joy.

"I knew, Lukas, I knew when day came all would be clear."

Lukas gazed around speechless. He had not realised how many glaciers gripped the sides of the mountains. The one they had traversed was close by where they stood, sparkling in the sunrise as if on fire, and its surface looked smooth and easy to cross, whilst ahead the path led down towards the grasses of the lower slopes. He had seen beauty in his own land, but here the ethereal quality of the light magnified the splendour so that the landscape surpassed anything he had ever witnessed.

"Come," cried Galen, "follow me."

Their steps were swift and eager now as, with bursting hearts, they travelled rapidly over the ground. Galen stared constantly ahead waiting for the moment when he would see the sweeping grandeur of the plain. Lukas gazed with him, searching unknowingly for a sign that they were nearing their destination. At last, as they rounded a wide corner, Galen saw beneath him the view he feared he had lost for ever.

"There, look!"

They stood side by side, tall and fine, their curls glistening in the sunlight. Below them stretched the plain and across it flowed the River and, towering in the middle, solitary in its unchanged glory, reared the Tree. Galen turned his shining face to his companion.

"The Tree, it stands there still."

Awestruck, Lukas shook his head in wonder.

"I knew of it, I have read about it as a myth of aeons ago, but thought it merely a dream born of a long-lost innocence."

"How could I have left it?" Galen's voice was hardly audible. "All I needed to know lies within the shelter of its branches."

"The fruit?" The question slipped out of Lukas's mouth before he was fully conscious it was in his mind.

"The fruit hangs beneath the boughs, succulent and golden. It must never be touched."

Lukas looked at Galen, a long look in which he remembered the story Claire had told him late that night of the apple she had offered Galen in the kitchen.

Galen understood his troubled silence.

"Do not remind me! I am nearly home again and the Tree stands waiting. I have paid the price for my weakness; the terror I suffered on your side of the wall could not be imagined by any of my people." He calmed himself and gazed at the Tree through half-shut eyes. "Jedra was right and I was mistaken. I thought I had the right to know. But all will be well, for the Tree is still there unchanged, the River flows across the plain, and the life of my people will continue to be held in the eternal harmony of the Tree's wide shelter and the water's song."

Lukas smiled with pleasure at Galen's words.

"What will your people do when they see me with you?"

"They will love and accept you, for their hearts are filled with nothing but love. Come, let us hurry."

"The whole plain is touched with a special light." Lukas was whispering. "Oh, Galen, it's so beautiful, I'm afraid to tread on such sacred ground."

"We have to cross for this is the only way home to my people but, do not be afraid, it has been trodden upon many times by many different feet."

Down they hurried, seeing nothing but the great plateau below, and they never paused or spoke until they stepped upon the plain and breathed its sweet scent and heard, close by, the River's call and gazed up at the Tree soaring towards the light above, massive in its towering majesty, its gigantic trunk rooted deep within the earth. Galen was the first to express their joint thought.

"We will go around the edge of the plain, and wait to approach the Tree until we have spoken with my people."

Lukas nodded. The beauty of the Tree was overwhelming

and he could look upon it no longer, for the glory he encountered made his heart beat so fast he could hardly breathe. His face was whiter than ever and the pale skin glinted with perspiration. Galen's features were blanched almost to transparency and his mouth trembled.

They crossed the plain as quickly as they could, taking a less direct route so as to put as wide a distance as possible between them and the Tree. Even so, the long shadows from its branches appeared to follow them and jump into their path so that, however circuitous their way, they could not escape its leafy patterns and, every now and then, an imprint of its fruit lay at their feet, making them stumble.

Across the plain they travelled, tiny upon its green expanse, walking close together and gasping in their haste to cover the ground. The River swept across the land, disappearing into an unknown distance, and they could feel its cool touch as they sped along.

"Hurry," urged Galen and they increased their pace, trying not to look at the ground and its shadows, or towards the Tree that seemed to follow them with its wooden grasp. Lukas began to think that they would never reach the far side and that their journey would end here in the vastness of an unknown yet disturbingly recognised world.

"How much further?" he gasped.

Galen did not reply but stared ahead with fierce concentration. On and on they tramped as the sun grew ever hotter and the very air seemed to breathe the thumping of their heavy heartbeats.

At last Galen pointed ahead and gave a great shout. There lay a valley with slender willows on either side and a path that wound away into the distance.

"Oh!" he cried in joy as the trees swayed towards him and the grasses sparkled with promise. "We are drawing near." Neither spoke of their relief to be across the plain, but both felt the constriction around their chests easing as they left it further and further behind. Up the valley they climbed and out onto rolling land that melted into the cultivated fields until, at last, they were passing through the wood that blinked its long drops of light onto their heads. Galen gripped Lukas's arm. "When we are through here, we are almost home."

Lukas nodded, unable to speak.

And so they emerged to where the meadows flowed quietly, and ahead they saw the low-lying buildings just as Galen had seen them not so many days before when he returned with the children from the early morning visit to the Tree. As the two men drew closer, the great Centre of Worship rose into view, shining in the brilliant light. Taking Lukas's hand Galen wept openly, overcome by the familiar and treasured sight. Lukas gazed in wonder even as the responsive tears fell from his own eyes.

"Why, what place is this? It's like nothing I've ever seen."

"You will see, you will meet my family, my people, and you will begin to understand, but for now we must go quickly."

They walked together along the silent paths until they reached the doors of the Centre of Worship. Here they paused whilst Galen listened intently. For a moment he looked puzzled.

"I must have been mistaken; it is later than I thought. The people are about their daily tasks, but I am sure my wife Anna will still be at home; we will go and find her."

Lukas moved with Galen, but he looked about him with increasing apprehension.

"I have never known such absolute silence, it doesn't seem natural. There's something about the beauty and the stillness here that frightens me. I have felt it ever since we stepped onto the plain. What's happening, Galen?"

Galen did not reply for he was hurrying ahead eagerly towards his own home.

"I am home," he cried, and started to run. "Anna, Anna, I am returned!" The door stood wide open, but no figure came to the door to greet him. "Anna! Anna, are you here?"

The two men waited breathlessly for an answering call, but none came.

"Do you think we should go in?" whispered Lukas, but Galen did not move, only cried the name of his wife again and again with increasing urgency.

They waited for a long time whilst the calls' echoes died away and the air was silent once more. When the figure moved into the doorway they could not stir, so great was their tension and surprise. Anna was more beautiful than ever.

"Galen." Her face flushed deep red like the fruit she held in her hand. "I am so glad you have come. See, when I awoke today this apple lay beside me on the pillow where your head should rest. It must be returned to the Tree, but I cannot take it alone. Now you are both here, we may go together." She did not seem surprised to see Lukas for she smiled at him as if she knew him, and he returned her smile.

"Where are the children, where are the people?" Galen gazed in horror at the apple in her hand.

"Ask no questions, you must ask no more questions. See, the apple is untouched. Take it and go with me to the Tree."

Stepping back, Galen shook his head vehemently.

"Put it down, Anna." His mouth was parched with the effort of speaking. She did not obey and her eyes glinted as she beseeched her husband to draw near. Still he remained motionless, his hands clenched by his side, his own eyes drier than dust. Into the space between them stepped Lukas, holding out his hand.

"Give me the apple, Anna, I am not afraid of it."

"Do not touch it!" cried Galen, but it was too late for Lukas's fingers curled around the fruit whilst Anna smiled at him in gratitude.

"Quickly, let's go," she said and Lukas nodded, impatient to get the deed done. "Come, my husband."

Galen did not move.

"Where are the children, where are my people? Nathan came to meet us, where is he?"

"Ask no questions now, Galen, we must go."

Still he did not move. He stood beneath the glaring sun and threw back his head and howled in grief. Lukas and Anna sped to his side.

"Come, come," they implored but, even as they spoke, a giant shadow fell across them, blotting out the light and casting them into chilling darkness.

"Look!" Lukas pointed in horror.

Towering over them was the Tree, massive in its brooding silence, its arms stretching wider than the farthest buildings. It arched over them, a huge and frowning presence, the fruit hanging from its branches like balls of burning blood. In the middle of the lower leaves, a savage gap exposed the place where the apple had been wrenched away.

"Put back the fruit!" cried Anna to Lukas.

"I cannot!" He stretched out the claw of his hand to Galen. "Help me."

But Galen did not speak or move. He gazed up at the Tree with empty eyes.

Anna ran to Lukas and, in her despair, she raked his head with her nails, so that the crimson clung to his brow, even as the fruit in his hand dropped to the ground.

Galen moved at last.

"The Tree," he whispered, holding his arms wide in agony.

The Tree was shrinking, disintegrating even as they gazed in fascinated horror.

"Run," cried Lukas taking Anna by the hand, "run!"

It was too late. Before they could move the stones began to fall upon their heads, forcing them to their knees as the wall crashed down on top of them, burying them beneath the weight of its granite force.

ɪ

# Protaph

The wind blows sweetly across the plain, ruffling the grasses so that the greens shimmer and scent the air with flowers. The very emptiness emphasises the vast expanse and nothing moves above the land's flat surface but the sky.

The wind blows and the ice-pure song of the River flows unchecked across the open spaces. Far away hang the glaciers and, over them, the mountain peaks sharpen their summits against a boundlessness of blue.

The way to the plain will be found by passing amongst the woods where light glances in, across the undulating pathways and through the valley of slender trees. It will follow the path of the sun and the scent of the water. There will be no other way.

The Tree rises up out of the middle of the plain, holding out its arms in invitation to those who come to rest against its ancient breast, its renewing bark. No eyes have ever seen the topmost branches, but an infinity of gazers have looked upon the fruit which hangs in untouched succulence amongst the leaves.

The Tree stands alone upon the plain. Only the River can sing to it the song of tomorrow, or yesterday, the tune of eternity.

The wind blows sweetly, but the branches of the Tree never stir, and the fruit hangs golden in its waiting stillness.